MOONLIGHT MASQUERADE

MOONLIGHT MASQUERADE

•

Amanda Harte

AVALON BOOKS
NEW YORK

PRINTED IN THE UNITED STATES OF AMERICA
ON ACID-FREE PAPER
BY HADDON CRAFTSMEN, BLOOMSBURG, PENNSYLVANIA

For three very special New Jersey women:
Marie Buglione
Martha Finch
Colleen McNally
I'm so lucky to have you as friends!

Chapter One

There were worse things in life. After she slipped
on the green satin mask, all she had to do was walk
though the door and hand her cape to the attendant.
That's all. Steps one and two were simple. Then there
was number three: not simple, not at all. For the twen-
tieth time that evening, Judith Barlow wondered what
had possessed her to invent such an insane scheme.
Why would a woman who had only recently outgrown
terminal shyness come to a party filled with strangers?

Tonight wouldn't be so bad, she told herself firmly.
At least she had the mask. With that covering half her
face, it was unlikely anyone would recognize her. Next
time she wouldn't have the mask, which was why she
was here. Tonight was the dress rehearsal, her chance
to perfect the role. If she could make it through the
evening without anyone discovering her masquerade,
she'd be ready for prime time—literally.

Judith's hands began to shake as she thought of the television interview that was now only days away. Why on earth had she agreed to it? *She* hadn't, she reminded herself. Lynette Thomas had. And Lynette would be a huge success—of course she would.

With her head held high in an imitation of bravery she was far from feeling, Judith laid her velvet cloak on the counter and walked into the ballroom.

"Let me guess who you are." A man dressed as Long John Silver approached her before she had taken three steps into the room. Judith tried to smile. The former mansion was the perfect setting for a Halloween party, with orange and black streamers draped from the chandeliers and dozens of real pumpkins carved with an amazing variety of expressions. She inhaled the scents of fresh flowers, expensive perfumes, and candle wax.

Long John nodded as if he recognized her, while a disc jockey struggled to be heard over the buzz of conversation. "You're Napoleon's Josephine." Though one eye was covered with a black patch, the other was carefully scrutinizing her costume.

Judith tried not to blush. The gown was beautiful. Its sea-foam green silk was designed to highlight deep green eyes and provided the perfect foil for strawberry blond curls. With its high waistline, slim skirt, and the delicate ruching that edged the hem and decorated the tiny puffed sleeves, it was a dress any Regency heroine could have worn to Almack's with pride. Though it was the perfect gown for Lynette, it was far different from the tailored suits that Judith wore to work and the jeans and sweatshirts that constituted her weekend wardrobe. It was no wonder, she told herself, that she still felt awkward in it.

Judith shook her head at Long John. "I'm not Josephine." With a slight curtsey, she introduced herself. "Pleased to meet you, milord. I'm Lady Emilie Wilshire." Even to Judith's critical ears, her English accent sounded authentic. Now if only she could remember it for the rest of the evening.

For the first time the man's uncovered eye rose above her collar bones, and she could see the question in it. "Don't believe I've heard of her."

"She's a character in a book," Judith said, as she accepted a miniature quiche from one of the circulating waiters. *My book*, she added silently.

"What do you think?"

Glenn Hibbard turned at the sound of his sister's voice. "I think you owe me for this. Big time." He gave Karen a calculating smile. "I'm thinking about a week at a Hilton Head condo. After all, that was slave labor I just did." Glenn had never been one to say no when Karen asked a favor, but tending bar—even on a temporary basis—while dressed in a Halloween costume was beyond the call of duty. Particularly this costume.

"How about theater tickets as soon as I finish paying for this bash?" Karen wrinkled her nose at the thought of the caterer's bill.

Glenn laughed, knowing he would never collect. It wasn't just that he earned considerably more than his sister. The fact was, neither a resort condo nor Broadway tickets held much appeal to a man alone. "Whatever this is costing, I think it's safe to say your guests are enjoying the party." Glenn looked around the room. Though he had to admit it was a bit odd to see a witch dancing with a green dragon, not to mention a scarecrow and a hoop-skirted belle trying to relive the sixties with a version of the twist, from the number of people who wore grins as well as costumes, Glenn was certain his sister's party was a success.

The Halloween bash was an annual event for her, and each year she had entreated him to come East for it. But Michelle hadn't liked the idea of a masquerade, and so Glenn had pleaded distance as their excuse. Now that he was alone and lived thirty rather than three thousand miles from Karen, he'd had no reason to refuse.

"How about you, little brother? Are you enjoying yourself?"

Glenn grinned mischievously. "Bartending was never my forte. On the other hand, if you'd like to introduce me to the prettiest girl in the room, I might consider forgiving you."

"Would you forget about the condo?"

"Not a chance."

"Then you're on your own. Use that famous Hibbard charm and find yourself a date. There's bound to be a Brandi or Tammi or Susi just waiting for you to whisper sweet nothings in her ear."

That was what he wanted, wasn't it? A harmless flirtation with no promises, no commitments, nothing to remind him of what might have been. An hour later, after he'd danced with half a dozen women, Glenn began to reconsider. The costumes varied, the hair colors differed, and the voices bore slightly different accents. The conversation, however, was predictably the same: boring. It had been a long time since Glenn had been bored. He hadn't enjoyed it then, and he certainly wasn't enjoying it now.

This wasn't the way the evening was supposed to turn out. The party had seemed like the perfect opportunity to launch the new Glenn Hibbard. He had a new job, a new home. Now he needed new friends. Admittedly, he hadn't been thrilled about wearing a costume. And when Karen informed him that the only costume left in his size was a knight in shining armor, Glenn's enthusiasm had plummeted again. Who wanted to sound like a pile of clanking tin cans every time he moved? Still, a masked ball had some advantages, or so he'd thought. Now he wasn't so sure. If the women were all like the ones he'd just met, he would have been better off staying home. Even sitcom reruns had more variety.

Slowly Glenn made his way toward the terrace door. Karen had told him that one of the reasons she had selected the mansion for her party was that it had a terrace along one side. "If the evening's warm enough," she had explained, "couples will go out there to talk."

Raised eyebrows had been Glenn's only reaction. If this was anything like the parties he remembered, the reason for going out onto a secluded moonlit terrace was not to talk, although the preferred activity did involve lips.

The outside air was cool and crisp, a welcome change from the overheated room. He walked briskly to the far end of the brick patio, leaned his back against the railing, and closed his eyes. For the first time since his plane had landed at Newark, he questioned his judgment. Had he made a mistake coming East?

As she whirled from one partner to another in a high-spirited if not particularly authentic version of a square dance, Judith caught a glimpse of the line of dancers reflected in the mirrored wall. There was Long John Silver again, his patch now covering the other eye. Next came a witch linking arms with a surgeon. Tonight must be the night for doctors, for there was another physician, his stethoscope tucked into the pocket of his white uniform. And there was a red-headed woman in a beautiful green dress.

Judith's eyes widened in shock, and for the briefest of instants, her feet refused to obey the commands her brain sent. It was true! She recovered quickly, taking an extra skip to catch up with her partner. She managed to finish the dance by focusing her attention on the intricate steps. But as soon as the reel was over, her eyes flew back to the mirror. There was no mistake. *She* was the red-haired stranger.

It just might work. With the curly strawberry wig, green contact lenses, and the gorgeous gown, she bore little resemblance to the woman the employees at the

Sixth National Bank knew. That woman had light brown hair, gray eyes, and was never seen without either her glasses or one of her conservatively tailored suits.

For the first time since the charade had started, Judith began to feel confident. Unless her eyes were deceiving her, it was possible that no one would learn that Lynette Thomas, author of a best-selling Regency romance, was none other than Judith Barlow of the bank's information systems department.

"Would you like a glass of punch?" the doctor who had been next to her in the reel asked.

"Something cool would be delightful," Judith replied, giving her words Lynette's slight English accent. Each time she spoke, it was easier to remember the accent. That was part of the reason for attending the party: to practice Lynette's voice and mannerisms. And since she would never see these people again, there was no real danger if she made a mistake.

When the doctor returned with her drink, he gestured toward the door. "It's cooler out there, and it's bound to be a lot quieter."

Judith nodded. When they reached the door, she started to open it, then stopped. Lynette would wait for a man to open doors for her. In fact, Lynette would probably expect him to lay down his coat like Sir Walter Raleigh. If the masquerade was going to work, she had to do more than speak like Lynette; she had to become Lynette.

The terrace stretched the length of the hall. Bounded on one side by the building and the other by a wooden balustrade, it was perhaps ten feet wide. In the summer, Judith suspected, there would be chairs and tables, hanging plants, and potted flowers out there. Tonight there was nothing.

When they had walked only a few feet, the doctor stopped and pointed to a small gazebo in the distance. Judith leaned against the railing and looked at the grounds. In season they were probably lovely, but this evening not even her active imagination could provide a reason for gazing at the landscape. Though it was indeed quiet on the terrace, that was the only inducement she could find for being outdoors.

"Lynette."

As the doctor touched her shoulder, she turned to face him. A little scintillating conversation or even some not so brilliant dialogue would be a pleasant change from dancing, sipping punch, and making small talk.

The doctor had other ideas.

In a movement so quick she had no way of anticipating it, he jerked her into his arms and began to kiss her. Judith's reaction was instinctive. With a motion as swift as the doctor's own, she slapped his face.

As the doctor howled in pain, a man laughed.

Chapter Two

How dare he? It was bad enough that someone had witnessed that scene, but how could he laugh? Judith clenched her fists, then gathered her remaining shreds of dignity and turned toward the building. It was time to leave; the party was no longer fun.

"How can I ever repay you?" The man's voice was closer than his laugh had been. Though she had believed him to be at the far end of the terrace, he was obviously walking in her direction. When the doctor had stormed back into the ballroom, Judith thought the bystander would disappear as well. After all, the show was over.

"You saved me from a fate worse than death."

Judith halted in midstride. Whatever she might have expected him to say, it wasn't that. Her eyes widened in surprise as the man reached her side, and for a moment she forgot the doctor's unwelcome kiss as she realized that this man's laughter had not been directed at her. He was laughing *with* her.

"That's supposed to be my line, isn't it?" she asked as she recognized his costume. "After all, you're the knight in shining armor. You're the one who's supposed to do the rescuing."

Though the light was dim, she could see that he was tall, red-haired, and broad-shouldered, with a firm chin. The rest of his face was hidden behind the mask, but—using the criteria she'd employed all evening—Judith guessed he was reasonably good-looking. What she knew for certain was that he had an engaging laugh.

There was more than a hint of mirth in the man's voice as he spoke. "You, fair damsel, were obviously well able to defend yourself."

As a light breeze stirred the air, Judith shivered. Her gown was not designed for autumn evenings.

"Do you want to go back to the party?"

She shook her head. Even though she doubted the doctor would bother her, the evening had lost its charm. All she wanted was to be somewhere, anywhere, else.

It was almost as though the red-headed knight could read her mind. "Would you like to go someplace for dinner? Those hors d'oeuvres weren't my idea of a meal."

Impulsively, Judith nodded. And so they had come to one of the small diners for which New Jersey was famous. Good food, fast service, and, as Judith could now attest, no questions. While Lutèce or indeed almost any white tablecloth restaurant would have at least raised an eyebrow when two oddly costumed people asked for a booth, the diner's hostess had seemed oblivious to their dress. Her only question had been whether they wanted the nonsmoking section.

Judith herself had more questions. She leaned forward, resting her arms on the pea green Formica table and trying to ignore the way it clashed with the blue Naugahyde seats. "What was the fate worse than death?" she asked.

As the man who had introduced himself as Glenn Hibbard stared at her blankly, she noticed that his eyes were a deep blue. Though she had expected green because of his auburn hair, it had been difficult to tell on the terrace or in the car as they'd driven to the diner.

"You mean you've forgotten?" Judith smiled, remembering how the outrageous comment had deflected her anger, turning it to mirth. "You thanked me for saving you from it . . . whatever it was."

Glenn laughed, an infectious sound that invited Judith to join him. "Oh, that." He shrugged his shoulders, then winced as the armor scraped his neck. "I was bored out of my skull."

"And I provided the entertainment." Judith kept her syllables neatly clipped, hoping that her accent sounded authentic. She'd introduced herself to Glenn as Lynette, and—according to the story she'd constructed—although Lynette had been in the States for several years, she still had a slight English accent.

The waitress placed oversized platters in front of

them, offering Glenn a bottle of catsup from another table.

"I thought you would have ordered lamb chops," Glenn said as he eyed Judith's plate.

"We English do eat things other than lamb." Apparently her accent was convincing, for he seemed to have accepted her as British. "Gammon, for example." She gestured with her fork toward the ham steak, then reminded herself not to shift the fork back to her right hand. For weeks she'd practiced keeping the fork in her left hand as the English did. That had proved to be almost as difficult as learning to drink tea, but eventually she'd mastered both.

"Do you work, Lynette?" Glenn asked, after he'd swallowed a bite of French fry. Then, as though afraid she might take offense at his question, he added, "Outside the home, I mean."

Judith noticed that he smiled as he looked at her left hand. Was that because she wasn't wearing a ring? She had glanced at his hands, too, and had seen that their only ornament was a signet ring on his right hand. Not that this was conclusive proof of bachelorhood, not that it mattered. She would never see him again after tonight, for tomorrow she'd go back to being Judith Barlow. Unlike Lynette Thomas, Judith Barlow was not a person who spent evenings in diners with complete strangers. The only times Lynette would reappear would be carefully orchestrated public appearances, like next week's Stockton show.

"Yes and no," she said in reply to Glenn's question. "I do work, but it's at home. I'm an author." It was the first time she had said that to anyone other than her best friend, Melinda, and it still felt strange to pronounce the words. Writing had been a dream for so long that it was difficult to realize it was now reality.

One of the other patrons started the jukebox, playing a popular country ballad.

"A published author?" Glenn raised his voice to be heard over the music. His faintly skeptical tone told Judith her answer had surprised him.

She nodded, and a faint blush rose to her cheeks. Would she ever become so accustomed to it that she could take her success for granted? Maybe in a hundred years or so.

"My first book is on the stands now," she said, cutting another piece of ham. The action gave her a reason to drop her gaze. Maybe Glenn wouldn't notice how uncomfortable she was talking about her career. She doubted he would understand what a thrill it had been to see the woman in the next line at the supermarket pick up a copy, read the back cover blurb, and actually buy it. Judith had come a long way from the shy little girl who had created imaginary playmates to the woman who, on a dare, had sent her manuscript to a New York editor. But there were still times— many times—when she thought she had invented her success the way she had her childhood friends.

Glenn tapped the bottom of the catsup bottle. "Would I have read your book?"

"Probably not," Judith admitted. She hesitated almost imperceptibly. It had been one thing to watch the woman buy her book. She had been anonymous then. This was different. How would Glenn react when she told him the type of novel she had written? Would he display the same uninformed scorn her boss did, equating romances with mindless pornography?

She would never see Glenn Hibbard again, so she might as well be honest. After all, tonight was a dress rehearsal for next week. Jonathan Stockton would ask more difficult questions than that.

Judith took a deep breath. "My book's considered women's fiction. It's a romance set in England during the Regency era."

As the catsup began to pour, Glenn looked up. "You're right that I wouldn't have read your story. I rarely read fiction, and I don't think I've ever read a romance."

There was no hint of condescension in his voice, and Judith let out the breath she hadn't been aware of holding. Though it shouldn't have mattered what he thought, somehow it did.

As Glenn nodded, the waitress refilled his coffee cup and brought Judith a fresh pot of water and another tea bag. When she left, Glenn turned back to Judith, his blue eyes sparkling with amusement. "If you tell me the title, I'll brave the raised eyebrows at the bookstore and buy a copy."

Oddly enough, Judith sensed that he meant it. She looked at him for a second, considering. "You could always wear your armor as protection." Though she hadn't expected it, for a few minutes Judith had forgotten that she was pretending to be Lynette. Glenn was such an enjoyable companion that she had relaxed and actually become Lynette, the shyness that had been her constant companion disappearing.

"Are you making fun of my costume?" His grin took the sting from his words. "Believe me, it wasn't my idea to be a knight in squeaking armor."

Judith looked down at her elegant gown, so different from her normally conservative clothing. "I wouldn't dare make fun of anyone's costume for fear they'd mock mine."

"Ogle maybe, but I doubt there'd be any mockery." Glenn dipped another French fry in the catsup. "Is your dress from the Regency period?"

Judith nodded. "I'm dressed as my heroine." She could feel Glenn's eyes once more studying her costume.

"I think I would have liked living during that time," he said with an appreciative glance at the neckline.

It was odd. If someone else had made the comment, she would have been annoyed, perhaps even angry. But there was something about Glenn's tone that kept her from taking offense at his words. She heard simple admiration in them.

"I doubt you would have enjoyed the clothes you'd have had to wear then," she countered. "The men wore even more outrageous things than the women. How would you like a high starched collar that scraped your face every time you turned your head or pants so tight you had to be sewn into them?"

Glenn paused, a bite of steak halfway to his mouth. "You mean there was something worse than armor?

Tonight was more than enough to convince me that I'm glad I didn't live during the Middle Ages."

"Not just that," Judith added. "There were worse costumes at the party. I can't imagine being inside that dragon's body all night."

Glenn laughed, and Judith noted the tiny creases that formed at the corners of his eyes. With his square chin and forehead and the straight line of his nose, Glenn's face was an angular one. The smile added a softness that she found attractive.

"Was the dragon male or female?" he asked. "I couldn't tell."

"Since we'll miss the unmasking, we'll never be certain."

Glenn glanced at his wrist. The multifunction digital watch was most definitely not part of his costume. "There's still time. Do you want to go back?"

"Not at all." The words came out more forcefully than Judith had intended, and she flushed slightly.

"Good, because neither do I. I'm enjoying being here too much."

"It is a good diner."

"The food has nothing to do with it. The company, on the other hand . . ."

As Judith flushed again, Glenn chuckled. "You've probably heard this a million times, Lynette, but your eyes turn even deeper green when you blush."

She shook her head. That was one line she'd never heard, for the simple reason that her eyes weren't green, any more than her hair was strawberry blond. It was only Lynette who had that coloring. Judith's was less flamboyant, just as her clothes were more conservative.

"Shall I turn the tables and ask if you work outside the home?" Judith asked. Perhaps if she kept the conversation on ordinary topics she would be able to forget the expression she'd seen in Glenn's eyes. He may have thought hers turned deep green when she blushed, but she knew beyond the shadow of a doubt that his had darkened when he looked at her.

He took a drink of his coffee, frowned, and added more cream. "I'm a consultant," he said.

If she had had to guess, she would have said he was a stockbroker. "Consulting's a pretty broad field. What's your area of expertise?"

"Management consulting. I work with a lot of firms that are downsizing or want to reengineer their processes." His armor clinked as he gave a deprecating shrug. "I guess you could say my expertise is in the latest management fads."

Judith nodded. Though she could not admit it, in her role at the bank she'd had numerous experiences with consultants who advocated what she called *trend du jour.* "Downsizing" and "reengineering" were among their favorite words.

"Are you an independent, or do you work for a firm?"

"I'm part of Lafland," Glenn said, naming one of the largest consulting firms in the country.

The waitress cleared their plates and handed them dessert menus.

"I just transferred here from the L.A. office," Glenn told Judith.

Los Angeles. That was another surprise. She wouldn't have picked him as a Californian. "How are you finding the transition?"

Glenn's blue eyes twinkled as he said, "A week ago I might have given a different answer, but I have to say that this is an improvement over L.A."

"No diners in California?" she asked, deliberately misunderstanding him.

"No beautiful redheads."

For years Judith had worked on perfecting her technique. At first she had used scathing comments to quell a young man's enthusiasm. Then she had discovered that a cold stare and a slightly raised eyebrow, which made no attempt to be anything but haughty, worked equally well. She was now master or, more accurately, mistress of the game. A stranger might try a suggestive comment or an overly friendly arm around the shoulder once. One had even dared a pat on the derriere as they walked out of a conference room. But no one who had experienced her disdain had ever tried a second time.

Tonight, though, she felt no need for defense mechanisms. She could rationalize it by telling herself she was no longer in a business setting. She could say that the warmth in Glenn's eyes was not threatening and that the diner's fluorescent lights kept the situation from being even remotely romantic. But all that was begging the question. The simple truth was that for the first time in a long while, she was enjoying a man's compliments. Knowing that she would never see him again had probably done more to destroy her inhibitions than consuming a bottle of brandy.

"A dreadful loss, I'm sure."

"Think of it this way. I can now indulge my fantasies."

"Oh, milord, I fear your revelations will wound my sensibilities." Judith deepened her accent and adopted the slightly querulous tone her heroine had used at the beginning of the book. She clasped her hands together in a parody of dismay. "Alas, I neglected to bring my smelling salts."

Glenn's smile turned into a full-fledged laugh. "That's why your knight in shining armor is close at hand. How did you know that one of my fantasies is to rescue a damsel in distress?"

"What if the damsel rescues herself?" Judith asked, recalling the scene on the terrace.

"Then we'll have to try again. You're the author—write me a rescue scene."

Judith narrowed her eyes slightly, appraising him. His shoulders were broad, his arms muscular. It didn't take much imagination to picture him as the hero of one of her books, sweeping the heroine into his arms and carrying her off to his castle.

"Are you interested in a stairway scene like *Gone With the Wind*?" she asked, then tried to banish the picture she'd just conjured. Why did she have to have such a vivid imagination? She didn't even have to close her eyes to see the tender expression on his face as he lowered his lips to the heroine's. *Think of something else, you fool*, she admonished herself.

"If you're considering that," she continued, trying to keep her voice from revealing her own fantasies, "I'm afraid I have bad news. Your armor will probably scratch the heroine."

Glenn looked down at the tin plates covering his torso. "I could always take it off," he suggested, reaching for the buckles that secured the breastplate to the back of the armor.

"That might shock our waitress."

"Well, then, there's only one thing to do. Let's find a more conducive spot. Your place or mine?"

They were back on familiar ground now. "I'm afraid I've heard that line before. Try again. I value originality."

"What if I begged on bended knee?"

"That's a bit more original," she admitted, "but your armor would probably squeak."

"That cursed armor again. There's only one thing to do."

"Order a piece of pumpkin pie." Judith signaled the waitress.

"Somehow, that wasn't what I was going to suggest."

"Somehow, I didn't think it was."

Judith had no sensation of time passing. All she knew was that the bantering continued, and if she had her way, it would never end. Glenn's repartee was quick, imaginative, and more than a little risqué. With another man, the same comments would have been offensive, but Glenn delivered them with such panache that, far from being insulted, she was complimented. Perhaps it was because he was open in his admiration. Whatever the reason, Judith was enjoying it.

"Excuse me." Their waitress stood next to the booth, and for once she did not have a coffee pot in her hand. "My shift is ending, and I need to close out your tab."

Glenn looked at his watch, his eyes widening in surprise. "It's three o'clock." They'd been sitting in the diner for five hours.

When Glenn had paid the bill and left the waitress a generous tip, he slipped Judith's cloak around her shoulders. "It's been a wonderful evening," he murmured.

As they reached the bottom of the stairs, Glenn turned. In one fluid motion, he slid an arm under her knees, the other around her back. Before she knew what was happening, Judith found herself cradled in his arms, her head resting on his chest.

She was wrong. The armor did not scratch.

Chapter Three

Judith tried to mask her impatience. After all, it was far from the first time Tony had tried this particular tactic. He would call her into his office, then ask her to wait while he made a series of phone calls, few of which were business related. Today he was discussing zero coupon bonds with his stockbroker while Judith leafed through the notes from their last meeting, trying not to frown. Tony might be rude, inconsiderate, and seemingly obsessed with his financial affairs, but he was her boss. And so she would pretend that his lack of consideration didn't bother her. She'd worked too hard to let Tony Walker's poor manners defeat her.

"Sorry, Judith," he said when he replaced the receiver. "I appreciate you coming in early this morning." His smile was ingenuous, as though he were unaware that he'd forced her to wait through fifteen minutes of phone conversations. It was a smile which, combined with his dark good looks, rarely failed to charm women. It failed utterly and completely with Judith.

"We've got an opportunity."

This time Judith did frown. "Opportunity" was Tony's euphemism for "problem."

"Lyle's called in some consultants," Tony said, referring to his boss. "There's no easy way to tell you this, but the bank is thinking about outsourcing your project. The consultants are supposed to do a study to see whether outsourcing DDA will save the company money."

Judith took a deep breath. This was not a good way to start Monday morning. No wonder Tony had left a message on her answering machine at home, asking her to meet him at 7:30.

"We already know that our DDA support costs are the lowest in the state," she pointed out. Judith herself had been part of a study two years earlier to compare her group's costs with those of other major New Jersey banks. They had found that Sixth National's demand deposit accounting system, DDA for short, was the most cost-effective. Oh, there was no doubt that demand deposits, as commercial checking accounts were called, cost more to process than personal checking accounts, but Judith's group had minimized those charges.

"You know that, and I know that," Tony said as he pulled a sheet of paper from a manila folder. He frowned at it, then laid it back on his desk. Judith's eyes widened slightly. Surely it was only her imagination that Tony's hand seemed to tremble. "Someone has told Lyle that outsourcers can do it cheaper," he said.

Outsourcing. It was one of those dreaded *trends du jour* that consultants seemed to espouse. Just the word was enough to make grown men break into a sweat, for it conjured up images of layoffs and unemployment lines.

"No one has been successful outsourcing DDA." Though Judith knew she was grasping at straws, she had to try. She looked at the window behind Tony's desk. Odd—the day was still as sunny and beautiful as when she'd driven to work. It was only Tony's announcement that made it seem as if it should be rainy and dismal.

"You know that, and I know that," Tony agreed. "But Lyle is convinced that we can be the ones to show the industry how to do it the right way."

"And in doing that we put half a dozen people out of work." That was the problem. Senior management and consultants spoke of profitability and bottom lines. They seemed to forget that people's lives were affected.

"Now, Judith, you know that the bank has a policy of retaining its best employees. You can count on me. I'll go to bat for you." Tony leaned across the dark walnut desk, a solemn expression fixed on his face. She'd seen that look before. On those rare occasions when his smile failed to charm, he adopted an earnest mien. It was supposed to inspire confidence, but in Judith's case, it had the opposite effect. The one thing she knew was that she could not depend on Tony to defend her or her staff.

"Besides, if you do your job right, we won't outsource, and I'll be able to recommend your promotion." Judith sighed. This was vintage Tony, wielding both a carrot and a stick. He knew how hard she had worked for the promotion. It should have been approved last year, but the bank had had a moratorium on promotions to Officer. Now that the ban had been lifted, Judith had hoped her new title would be confirmed effective January 1. The outsourcing study could change all that.

"The consultants are going to be here at ten," Tony said. "I've scheduled lunch in the executive dining room at twelve." His eyes narrowed as he looked at Judith, scrutinizing every detail of her appearance, apparently trying to see her as the consultants would.

Surely he could find no fault with her clothing. She was wearing one of her usual conservatively cut suits. Today it was a light gray that highlighted her eyes. With her white silk blouse and darker gray pumps, it was the perfect banker's uniform. Even her glasses, a pale tortoiseshell that complemented her light brown hair, were far from flamboyant. The only incongruous note, and it was one Judith doubted Tony would see, was her ring. There was no way that could be considered conservative, for the exquisitely cut cameo was set in a heavy gold filigree that proclaimed it to be a valuable antique.

"Thank goodness you know how to dress," Tony said. Judith tried to suppress her annoyance that the man would question her common sense. When had she ever worn anything that wasn't eminently conservative . . . dull, in fact? *Saturday night*, a little demon replied. That green gown wasn't exactly bankers' garb. Judith schooled her features into a pleasant, noncommittal smile and forced away the images of a different kind of Saturday knight. That was another time and place, and she'd been another person then.

Almost as though he could read her thoughts, Tony picked up a magazine from the corner of his desk. "I can't believe some women," he said. "There's an article in here about a convention of lady writers. What a bunch of airheads they must be. They write stuff that's no better than pornography, and now some of them are even going out in public dressed like characters from their books." As he shook his head, his handsome face registered disgust. "It's kids' stuff. My sisters gave up games like that before they were six years old."

Judith could feel the blood drain from her face. It wasn't the first time she'd heard Tony's diatribe on women authors. Ever since he'd learned that some successful romance writers earned more money than he did as vice president of a major bank, he seemed to have launched a one-man crusade, ridiculing them at every opportunity.

At first she'd tried to reason with him, pointing out that he shouldn't judge books he hadn't read, but if there was one thing Judith knew about her boss, it was that once he formed an opinion, nothing—particularly not facts—would change it. And so she'd learned to bite her tongue and pretend she didn't care. But of course she did, for Tony's scathing criticism, even though it was based on blind prejudice, hurt. While he had no way of knowing it, Judith viewed it as a personal attack, since she was part of the group he scorned.

Someday she would tell Tony just how ridiculous his allegations were. But not today. Today she needed to prepare for an attack of a different kind. For it wasn't only her job that was jeopardized by outsourcing. It was also the jobs of the three people in her group who needed paychecks just as badly as she did. Matt had a wife and two small children. Sam was newly married with a large mortgage, and Betsy had dreams of someday owning her own home. Outsourcing could change all that.

Two hours later, Judith and Tony were seated in one of the bank's first-floor conference rooms, waiting for the consultants to arrive. Here, unlike the spartan rooms designed for employees' use, the furniture was mahogany and the carpet plush. No expense had been spared in the rooms bank customers might see.

Judith rose and nodded a greeting as the first two men entered the room. When the third appeared, her eyes widened and her heart began to thud.

Oh, no.

It couldn't be.

It was.

"And this is Glenn Hibbard, who'll be leading the study." The partner-in-charge completed his introductions. The man who had sat opposite her in a tacky diner booth, laughing and joking about his coat of armor, the man with whom she'd flirted shamelessly, the man who knew her as Lynette, took his place at the head of the table.

Why me?

Until thirty seconds ago, Judith had not believed in Fate. Now she had no doubts. Not only was there a Fate, but it had a strange sense of humor. How else could you explain the odds of ever seeing Glenn Hibbard again? One in a million? One in a billion? He'd said he was a consultant, but there were hundreds—maybe thousands—of consultants in the state of New Jersey. What kind of cruel Fate had made him the one who was conducting her bank's study?

Judith fixed a smile on her face, hoping it looked polite, disinterested, and totally different from the smile Lynette had worn. As she shook hands with Glenn, she noted, as she had only thirty-six hours earlier, that his hands were large and firm, with square-tipped fingers. Though he was wearing a blue pin-striped suit instead of armor, she would have recognized him anywhere. Tall, handsome, red-haired men were not an everyday occurrence.

The question was whether he recognized her.

You don't look at all like Lynette, she rationalized as she took her seat and glanced at the agenda Glenn had distributed. *You don't sound like Lynette*, she continued in her internal pep talk. *Most important, he's not expecting to see Lynette here. He won't recognize you.*

"Judith is my right-hand man, if you'll pardon the

expression," Tony told the consultants. "She's responsible for the DDA system and will be your primary contact during the study."

Judith tried not to think of how many hours she would be spending with Glenn if this study lasted the six to eight weeks that Tony had predicted.

Somehow she would get through those weeks; somehow she would ensure that Glenn had no reason to connect her with Lynette. For now it was not just important, it was critical, that no one at Sixth National know that Lynette and Judith were one and the same woman.

When she'd first sold *Golden Web*, Judith had insisted on using a pseudonym rather than face the bank's censure. Oh, she had known they wouldn't fire her. That would have brought adverse publicity, perhaps even a lawsuit, and those were two things any bank avoided. But she could forget that promotion; it would never be approved. In fact, given Tony's disdain for romance writers, it would never even be proposed.

Judith had seen what had happened to Sally Andress of the trust department, when the bank discovered that she worked nights as a waitress at a restaurant noted for the brevity of its costumes. Sally had been transferred to a back office job, where no one—certainly none of the wealthy customers who wanted to be sure their estates would be handled properly—would see her. A promising career had withered virtually overnight. Judith had no doubt that in the eyes of bank officials, writing a romance would be as heinous a crime as Sally's second job, and the promotion she had worked so hard to win would be lost.

Now with the possibility of outsourcing, the stakes were even higher. For the bank could end her job, claiming outsourcing as its reason, and she would have no recourse. If that happened, she would be virtually powerless to protect her team. The solution was clear: She had to keep Glenn and everyone at the bank from learning the truth.

"I'll need a copy of your departmental org chart and a list of all available documentation," Glenn told Judith when they had reviewed the agenda. "It's fairly important, so if we could have that by close of business tomorrow, I'd appreciate it."

Judith pulled a small sheaf of papers from her portfolio. "I think you'll find everything you need here." She kept her voice cool but polite, as different as she could make it from Lynette's joking warmth. That wasn't difficult. When she had taken assertiveness training years ago in an attempt to overcome her shyness, the facilitator had warned her that she would suffer relapses in moments of stress. Today certainly qualified as one of those.

"That's what I call efficiency," the partner said with a quick glance at the information.

Tony gave Judith an approving glance as he straightened his tie. "Our motto is 'Be prepared.' "

"I thought that was the Boy Scouts'. And"—Glenn looked directly at Judith—"unless I'm greatly mistaken, Ms. Barlow is no Boy Scout."

A round of laughter greeted his comment. Only Judith's face remained sober. He was simply trying to be friendly, to start the study on good terms, but she refused to smile. She wouldn't do anything to remind him of Lynette.

The next two hours passed quickly as they discussed the format of the study, with Judith hiding behind her coldest, most professional demeanor as though it were a protective shield. She answered every question politely and completely without ever injecting a note of humor. Not once did she respond to the openings Glenn gave her. Today she was as sober and humorless as Tony himself.

"Why don't you sit next to Judith?" Tony suggested to Glenn as they entered the dining room. "You two will be spending a lot of time together in the next couple months, so you ought to get to know each other."

There was no graceful way to avoid it.

"I'm hoping to make the study as painless as possible, given the subject." Glenn opened the menu.

"That's certainly an admirable goal." Had those words really come from her mouth? If one of her characters had used such stilted dialogue, her editor would have demanded a rewrite, and justifiably so.

Judith felt Glenn stiffen. Maybe it wasn't so bad. Perhaps her approach would work.

"It's just a study, you know. The outcome hasn't been decided."

If only that were true! But Judith held no illusions. When a company instituted a study like this one, it was usually because they had made a decision and wanted it corroborated by outside experts.

"Perhaps."

When the filet of sole arrived, Judith picked up her fork. Thank goodness she could eat with her right hand and drink coffee today! Judith doubted she could have carried off the charade of being British, not with the added strain of knowing her department's future hinged on the result of a study being conducted by none other than Glenn Hibbard. Knights were supposed to rescue damsels, not destroy people's careers. But Glenn was no more a knight than she was British.

Compared to Saturday evening, today should have been easy. Then she had been playing a role. Today she was only being herself. And yet when Judith left the office at the end of the day, she was exhausted. For some reason, being Judith Barlow was more difficult than pretending to be Lynette Thomas.

Something was wrong.

Something was wrong. As he drove home from the bank, Glenn frowned. Maybe things were different on the East Coast, but he doubted it. He'd conducted more than one outsourcing study, and none had begun as poorly as this one. It wasn't anything you could put your finger on. There was no overt sabotage, no obvious lack of cooperation. And yet something was wrong. His instincts told him that.

When the managing partner had told Glenn that the bank suspected embezzlement and that they were going to use the outsourcing study as a cover while they investigated, he had been skeptical. The controls banks had instituted years ago were highly effective; it was unlikely Glenn's team would uncover any irregularities. Now he wasn't so sure.

Glenn braked at the red light. The people at today's meeting had set his internal antennae to wiggling. Tony Walker was a little too jovial, his jokes a bit too forced. Glenn knew from experience that when a man in Tony's position was that friendly to a consultant, it was because he wanted something. In this case, perhaps it was only a recommendation that his job remain even if Judith's group was outsourced. But maybe it was something more sinister. Maybe he knew that there was a problem.

Judith Barlow was another story. No one could accuse her of being overly friendly. Did the woman ever smile, or was she afraid it would crack her face? Not that it was a bad face. Glenn entered the highway and merged with traffic. In her own way Judith was beautiful. Even the oversized glasses and the conservative hairdo couldn't disguise that. But cold! She gave new meaning to the term ice maiden. Working with her for the next two months was going to be no fun, no fun at all.

And then there was that ring she wore. Glenn very much doubted she had bought it on a banker's salary. It might have been a gift or something she had inherited. Then again, it might be one of the extravagances that so often revealed embezzlers.

As his car took the first exit, seemingly of its own volition, Glenn swore. This wasn't where he was sup-

posed to be. He should be home, preparing for tomorrow's meeting. It was absurd coming back here.
Only a total fool would imagine that Lynette would
be at the diner again tonight. Hadn't she told him she
was going back to England for an indefinite period?
Besides, why did he care? He'd gotten what he
wanted—a few hours of pleasant company with a
beautiful woman whom he'd never see again. No
promises, no commitments, no pain.

Why, then, did it seem so wrong?

Chapter Four

"I think I'm going to throw up."

Though the small dressing room was lined with mirrors, Judith kept her eyes firmly fixed on the table in front of her. The second last thing she wanted to do was see her reflection. Even the heavy makeup couldn't camouflage her pallor, and her hands shook like someone with a bad case of caffeine jitters. As for her stomach, the less said about that, the better. Nervous butterflies were one thing; she could deal with them. But tonight it felt as though a whole flock of buzzards were circling within her stomach, beating their wings against the sides.

"You are not going to throw up," Melinda said calmly. Judith swiveled the chair around and glared at her friend. "All you have is stage fright," Melinda continued in that maddeningly smooth voice. "You'll be fine as soon as you get in front of the cameras."

Judith gave her friend a scathing glance and rose to her feet. "And just when did you become such an expert on the therapeutic effects of television cameras?" she demanded as she walked toward the door. "As I recall, you've never had the pleasure."

"True," Melinda said, with an airy wave of her hand, "but I know you. You'll be fine."

"Of course I will," Judith agreed. When she saw a smile begin to cross Melinda's face, she added, "I'll be okay for the simple reason that I'm not going onto that stage."

She took a step toward the door. As she did, she caught a glimpse of herself in one of the long mirrors that lined the walls. Oddly enough, she looked perfectly normal. Judith would have sworn that terror was imprinted on her face, turning her features into an ugly caricature. Instead, if you could look beyond the theatrical makeup, it was Lynette Thomas's face that looked back at her. The strawberry curls and vibrant green eyes added softness to her classic features, a softness that was echoed in the delicate lace-trimmed jabot of her blouse.

She took another step toward the door.

"You wouldn't dare." Though Melinda's voice was soft, the deepening of her Southern accent told Judith she wasn't as calm as she appeared.

"Wouldn't I?" This time it was Judith who raised a skeptical eyebrow.

Melinda's blond curls bounced against her chin as she shook her head. "You can say whatever you want, but you're not going to miss the chance of a lifetime."

She swung her legs off the chaise longue and faced Judith, an unusually stern expression on her face. "You won't give this up, not when you know every writer in America would give her eyeteeth to be on that show. Didn't you tell me that when your editor heard Jonathan Stockton was going to feature artists on his special, she and every other publisher in the country begged, bribed, and threatened bodily harm to get one of their authors on the show?"

Judith shrugged, trying to forget the state of total euphoria she'd been in when her editor had told her Jonathan Stockton had asked her to appear on the show. Even authors whose books had made the best-seller list weeks before publication vied for a five-minute spot on the Stockton show. Yet Lynette Thomas, first-time author, had been selected for a segment on Stockton's annual special. The fact that the other guests included world-famous painter Paul Middleton and Vivian Ashton, generally regarded as the best young pianist in the country, only made Lynette's selection more significant.

"All Jonathan Stockton said was that his wife laughed and cried when she read your book, and that was enough for him," Judith's editor had reported, when she had asked why she'd been chosen.

Right now, Judith wasn't sure whether she wanted to laugh or cry. The only thing she was sure of was that she didn't want to set foot on that stage. It was one thing to sit at home thinking about how exciting actually meeting Jonathan Stockton would be. It was quite another to face those cameras and know her every word was going to be broadcast on national television.

Judith took another step toward the door.

"Coward!"

Judith glared at Melinda. She was *not* a coward!

"Perhaps you can explain to me," Jonathan Stockton said in the mellow voice that viewers all over the country had come to love, "where you get the inspiration for your feisty heroines. Isn't Emilie a twenty-first-century woman in nineteenth-century clothes?"

It was a question Judith had expected. "I wouldn't say so. If anything, I'd say that Regency women may have had fewer inhibitions than we do now." Emilie did things that Judith Barlow, conservative banker that she was, would only dream of. Emilie's life was so full of adventures that she had no time—nor the need—to invent stories with a heroine who always delivered the perfect witty reply rather than sitting tongue-tied and blushing when a man paid her a compliment or a woman criticized her clothing.

"Then Emilie's not based on you?"

"Oh, no." Judith smiled and gestured toward the book. "I'm nowhere near as brave as she is. I'd turn and run rather than endure some of the situations she finds herself in." That had been part of the fun of writing the book—putting Emilie in perilous positions and letting her get herself out of them.

Jonathan leaned forward, and his dark blue eyes met Judith's green ones. "Then you've never had to defend your virtue the way Emilie does several times during *Golden Web?*"

Judith shook her head. Her knight in shining armor had come when the need for rescue was gone. Of course, that was one story she had no inclination to share with tens of thousands of viewers. Glenn Hibbard might bear no physical resemblance to the hero of her book, but he lingered in her memory and disturbed her thoughts far more than her fictional heroes.

"Do you agree, Lynette?"

For the briefest of instants Judith looked at Jonathan Stockton blankly. What was the man talking about? Then she realized she'd missed his last question.

"That depends," she hedged.

When the studio audience roared, Judith knew her response was the wrong one. For the first time that evening Jonathan addressed the audience directly. "You be the judge," he said with an amused smile. "Lynette Thomas is either plotting a scene for her next best selling book, or else . . ." He lowered his voice a notch. ". . . she's thinking about her real-life hero."

Judith couldn't help it. She blushed.

East Coast, West Coast. The scenery might vary, but the food was the same. Glenn frowned as he pulled a package from the freezer and slid it into the microwave. At least when he'd been in California, he had worked regular hours. None of this coming home from the office so late that it was almost time for the ten o'clock news.

Glenn frowned again. It must be poetic justice that

he, a man who hated deception and lies, was working on an engagement under false pretenses. Though he had told Judith he was trying to measure the system's complexity, he had spent the evening poring over the system flow charts she had given him, trying to decide which programs were the most likely to contain the rogue code. As distasteful as it was to admit, someone—an insider—was becoming rich through a subtle but systematic scheme that auditors called a salami scam.

The theory was simple. Instead of stealing large sums, which would be quickly missed, the thief took tiny amounts, like thin slices of salami. The usual technique was to alter a rounding calculation. Instead of rounding to the closest penny, when the amount would have been increased, the penny was deposited in the perpetrator's account. The books remained in balance, and no one was the wiser. Unfortunately for this particular thief, the controller of one of the bank's largest customers was a stickler for detail and always checked his balances. When the same discrepancies occurred in three consecutive months, he notified the bank president. Glenn's "study" was the result of that call.

As the buzzer sounded the end of the cooking cycle and the smell of freezer cuisine filled the kitchen, Glenn pulled a bottle of mineral water from the refrigerator. Placing it and the now hot entree on a tray, he strode into the living room. Television might be a poor substitute for human companionship, but it sure beat silence. One thing was certain: He was not going to think about banks and embezzlers again tonight. Glenn reached for the remote control.

He was flipping through the channels, trying to ignore the fact that this dinner tasted like last night's, even though the box claimed it was a different meat, when he heard her voice.

"I like to make the distinction between fantasies and dreams," she said.

His pulse began to thud. It couldn't be. And yet it was. Sitting in what appeared to be a comfortable living room looking like she belonged there was the woman who had haunted his dreams for the better part of a week.

"Every woman has fantasies," Lynette Thomas continued. As she looked directly at the camera, those incredibly green eyes flashing with humor, Glenn's blood pressure reached new heights.

Fantasies. That was something he had learned a lot about since the night he'd spent in a diner with the woman who now appeared on his TV screen. It wasn't love, of course. Glenn wasn't foolish enough to believe that. Love was what he had felt for Michelle, and this was nothing like that. He had never joked with Michelle, and he most definitely had never carried her out of a diner. Michelle would not have been amused by that. Lynette Thomas was.

Glenn punched the "Record" button.

"What's more important than her fantasies are her dreams."

He knew about dreams, too. His dinner forgotten, Glenn leaned forward, resting his elbows on his knees.

I wonder what her fantasies are. His own focused on one sexy writer with strawberry blond curls and the greenest of eyes.

"A woman might fantasize about being swept off her feet by a knight in shining armor." Was she remembering how he'd held her in his arms? Even though he'd been wearing that ridiculous costume, he had savored the softness of her body as he'd cradled her to his chest. It had been over too soon, and yet the moment had fueled both his dreams and his fantasies.

"What she dreams about," Lynette continued, "is a man who'll laugh and cry with her, someone who'll be her best friend as well as her lover."

The talk show host looked pointedly at Lynette's hands. "Can I surmise by the fact that you're not wearing a ring that you haven't yet met the man of your dreams?"

Glenn knew he was not the only man in America who held his breath while he waited for her response. Lynette paused for a moment, smiling that lovely, provocative smile he'd seen in the diner. Then she said softly, "Shall we say that I continue to dream?"

At the commercial break, Glenn looked down. His dinner had congealed into a gray mess, and his stomach was protesting its long fast, but Glenn could not have cared less. At least now he knew he hadn't imagined Saturday night. The woman who had made him laugh more than anyone he'd met really existed. She wasn't simply a figment of his imagination.

As Lynette and the talk show host discussed feisty

heroines, Glenn started to chuckle. She certainly knew about them. Though she denied it, he didn't for a minute believe that she hadn't used herself as a model for her heroine. A woman who had handled that boor at the party the way she had and who was capable of the verbal sparring she'd traded with Glenn had firsthand experience with feistiness.

And then there was the moment when she had been lost in reverie, her face soft, her eyes misty as she thought about the man of her dreams. The lump in Glenn's stomach owed nothing to freezer cuisine and everything to the fact that no woman had ever looked at him with that expression. He had never seen that sweet smile on Michelle's face, not even the day they became engaged. Perhaps she had worn it for Jared.

Glenn jumped to his feet. He would not think about Michelle and Jared. They were the past, and he would not—absolutely would not—think about the past. The present was all that mattered.

He scraped his dinner into the disposal and grabbed a pint of ice cream. Wasn't chocolate ice cream the top of the food pyramid? Sitting in front of the TV once more, Glenn rewound the tape. *I wonder whether Judith Barlow was watching the show*, he mused as he hit the "Play" button. Shaking his head, he took a swig of water. Why had he thought of Judith? She certainly wasn't a romantic figure. Far from it. But feisty? You could call her that. It was obvious from the quiet but assured way she handled herself in meetings that she wouldn't let anyone take advantage of her. Glenn had the feeling that if Judith had encountered a man like the "doctor" at a party, she would have reacted exactly the way Lynette had. Of course, someone as sensible as Judith would not have gone to a costume party.

Why was he thinking of her, anyway? Lynette was the woman who starred in his dreams each night.

Chapter Five

"You're not really going to drink that vile stuff, are you?"

Judith sank back in her chair for a moment. "When you need caffeine as badly as I do," she said with a wry smile, "you'll even drink the bank's brew."

Raising one brow, Glenn looked pointedly at the Styrofoam cup sitting in front of him, untouched. "Some of us won't," he countered.

They were seated in one of the small conference rooms that project teams frequently used. Here there was none of the luxury that marked the executive offices. The tables were metal rather than wood, and the chairs were strictly utilitarian. The differences were not confined to the decor but also extended to the coffee service. Not only were there no china cups, but the beverage itself was far different. Judith's colleagues maintained that they were being treated to the famous ersatz coffee of the World War II era. On her more cynical days, Judith was convinced that not only was their theory about the recipe correct, but that the dark liquid in the carafe actually dated from the war.

She pushed back her chair and started to move toward the coffee. Glenn was right about its flavor. She had already had one cup that morning, and only desperation led her to consider another, a desperation caused by a night when sleep could be measured in minutes rather than hours. Though she had worn her favorite charcoal-gray suit today with a pink blouse that added much-needed color to her face, Judith knew the camouflage was only superficial. If she didn't keep a steady supply of caffeine in her bloodstream, her eyelids would droop.

"Late night working?" Glenn asked as Judith poured herself a cup of caffeine. There was no point in calling it coffee.

She shrugged. "What else?" It wasn't really a lie. She had been working; it just wasn't bank business that had kept her out until the early hours of the morning, although bank business was part of what had kept her from sleeping. The adrenaline that had been pumping through her veins after the Stockton show would have kept anyone awake. Combined with her worries about the outsourcing study, it was almost a miracle that she had slept at all.

Judith took a sip of the dark liquid, then wrinkled her nose. The coffee had not improved with time. Maybe if she regarded it as medicine rather than a beverage. . . .

"C'mon." Glenn stood up. "I saw a coffee shop across the street. Let's see whether they can make a decent cup of the stuff."

"But we have work to do," Judith protested. While she wasn't chained to her desk, it was unusual for anyone in her department to leave the bank except during lunch.

"So we take it with us." Glenn slid a few papers into his leather portfolio, tucked his pen into his shirt pocket, and reached for his suit jacket. "We can work just as well over there as here. Maybe better," he added. "At least there we have a chance of staying awake."

Judith quelled the small voice that told her this was dangerous. One of the things she had resolved while she lay awake was that she couldn't continue being rude to Glenn. This outsourcing study was painful enough without adding unpleasantness. Still, it was a giant leap from being polite to socializing with him.

"C'mon," Glenn repeated.

Judith grabbed her raincoat, pulling the hood over her head as she and Glenn left the bank. For once the weathermen had been correct, and the predicted heavy rains had arrived.

"Smells promising." Glenn made a show of sniffing the air in the small restaurant. The aroma of freshly brewed coffee blended with the tantalizing smells of baked goods. "Two coffees and Danish," he told the waitress, who had materialized at their table as soon as they were seated.

Judith wiped the raindrops from her glasses, then settled back in the chair.

"How long have you been at the bank?" Glenn asked when the coffee and pastries were delivered. Though he had laid his portfolio next to him on the table, Judith noticed that he made no move to open it.

"Six years," she answered. "Or, as some of my friends would say, two thirds of the way to vesting." Of course, if the outsourcing study ended the way she feared it would, she would never be fully vested. She and Matt and Sam and Betsy would meet in an unemployment office rather than their project room.

Clearly oblivious to her somber thoughts, Glenn chuckled. Judith felt herself stiffen. *Relax*, she urged herself. She knew there was no reason to blame Glenn. He hadn't initiated the study, and he wouldn't benefit, regardless of the results. Lafland was hired to perform the feasibility study, not to implement the outsourcing, if that was the recommendation.

"I never heard it phrased quite that way," Glenn said with a smile. "At Lafland we count years to partnership."

For a few minutes, he talked about his job. To Judith's silent amusement, Glenn described his career in far different terms than he had used Saturday night. Then he had focused on the personal aspects. Today he was purely professional, telling Judith about a number of prior engagements. It wasn't surprising. Men rarely found quiet Judith attractive enough to bother flirting with her. They confided in her as if she were a neighbor or a friend, not a woman. The fact that

Saturday night had been so very different—that a man had actually flirted with her and she had flirted back—was part of the reason Judith had found it wonderful.

Glenn was different today, and yet the man sitting across the table from her was as charming and attractive as the knight in armor had been. Doubts assailed her. She couldn't help making the comparison. What if Glenn did? What if he suddenly realized that she reminded him of the woman in the diner? Judith brushed her fears aside. If Glenn seemed so different to her when she knew who he was, it was highly unlikely he would make the connection between Lynette Thomas and Judith Barlow. He would have no reason to think of them together.

"Why did you come to New Jersey?" she asked, when Glenn had finished his tale of the hazards of consulting for a large pet store, including a runaway pot-bellied pig who had made his way into the conference room while Glenn was delivering the final report.

"I couldn't understand why everyone was laughing," he had said.

He wasn't laughing now. As he considered her question, Glenn's blue eyes clouded with what appeared to be pain, though he tried to mask it with a quick smile. Judith wasn't fooled. Whatever Glenn said, she was sure it would be at best only part of the story. There was bound to be another reason he had left California.

"My sister lives here," Glenn said smoothly. "She just went through a painful divorce."

"And so big brother came to help out." That could be the reason he looked so sad. Still, Judith's instincts told her the pain was somehow connected with California, and that it was more personal. Perhaps he had been married there. Perhaps his sister's wasn't the only divorce. She wouldn't ask, of course. Lynette might have asked such a personal question, but Judith would not.

"Little brother," Glenn corrected. He paused while the waitress refilled their cups. "How about you? Do you have siblings?"

Judith shook her head at his question, then nodded when the waitress offered a refill of coffee. "No family at all. I'm an only child, and my parents are dead." There was a moment of silence, when Judith sensed that Glenn was at a loss for words. "It was years ago," she said. Imaginary playmates had filled her childhood, and now Melinda was as close to a sister as she could have wished. Judith took a sip of coffee.

"Let me guess," Glenn said, with a glance at her hands as she placed the mug back on the table. "Your ring is a family heirloom."

Judith nodded, accepting the explanation he had proposed. It was only half a lie. The ring was an heirloom, all right. It just wasn't from her family. She had seen it in an antique shop when she'd been in England researching *Golden Web* and had fallen in love with it. Unfortunately, the delicate cameo was far beyond her credit limits, and so she'd left it behind. But when *Web* had sold, Judith had made an overseas phone call to London. Yes, the ring was still there. Ten days later it was on Judith's right hand. It had become almost a talisman, a silent reminder of her success in selling a book. Though no one at the bank knew of her other career, the ring was Judith's proof that *Web* was more than a dream.

With obvious reluctance, Glenn opened his portfolio, and for the next half hour they reviewed his list of questions and drank the coffee shop's excellent coffee.

"You've got all the answers," he said at one point.

If only that were true! Today Judith had no answers at all to what she and her team would do if the system were outsourced and they lost their jobs. "I've worked on the system for a long time," she said, in a voice that was amazingly calm. "I wasn't one of the original programmers—only Tony's left from that group—but after six years, I can practically quote the code verbatim."

Surely it was only Judith's imagination that Glenn found her statement so interesting. Did he think she was implying that she was irreplaceable and that outsourcing would never succeed? Judith took another sip of coffee and tried to change the subject. "What made you become a consultant?"

Glenn shrugged. "I'm not sure, really. Karen says it's because I'm obsessed with finding truth, and she claims that's what a consultant does."

The doorbell chimed as three teenage girls entered the coffee shop, announcing to anyone who would listen that the weather was not fit for humans. "I don't quite understand," Judith said when the girls were seated.

Propping his chin on one hand, Glenn regarded Judith steadily. "If you think about this study, everyone in your department wants me to think that DDA can't be outsourced, while the bank's senior management is convinced it should be. My job is to figure out where the truth lies."

There was the briefest of silences while Judith debated whether she wanted to know how accurate this Karen's assessment was. It made sense; it explained why Glenn appeared to enjoy his career so much and why he was successful at it. But if it were true, how would he react if he learned she had been playing a charade Saturday night, pretending to be someone she wasn't? Would he see that as deceit or recognize it for what it really was, an attempt at self-protection? It was, of course, only a rhetorical question, for there was no reason Glenn would ever know that Judith Barlow and Lynette Thomas were the same person.

Judith raised her eyes to Glenn's. "Are you? Obsessed, I mean."

As the jukebox began to blare a rock song, he shrugged again. "I wouldn't use exactly those words, but I do have a thing about people who lie." He looked directly at Judith, his deep blue eyes darkening. "It was one of the main reasons my sister and I fought as much as we did. I couldn't understand what she called little white lies, and she was sure I was a sanctimonious prig." He paused, then grinned. "I probably was."

* * *

"I won't lie to you." Judith leaned forward, making eye contact with each member of her team in turn. All three of them looked worried. "The consultants are here to evaluate DDA, to see whether it makes sense to outsource it."

"But we have the lowest costs in the state," Matt protested.

Sam's face whitened, and Betsy twisted her ring. Judith's eyes narrowed slightly. Unless she was mistaken, that was a new and very expensive ring on Betsy's right hand. The huge emerald flanked by good-sized diamonds sparkled too brilliantly to be a fake. Judith was surprised. Betsy's investment portfolio must be more profitable than Tony's if she was able to afford such an extravagant piece of jewelry.

"I know," Judith agreed with Matt. "The fact is, the bank wants to figure out whether they can save even more money."

"That's the bottom line, isn't it?" Sam's lip curled in disgust. "Money, not people."

Judith let them vent for a minute before she said, "It's only a study. There's no recommendation yet."

"But we know what it'll be," Sam said.

"Maybe not." Betsy spoke for the first time. "If we make it look really hard, maybe they'll decide they can't lose us."

Judith raised a cautioning hand. "I know how you feel, but we've got to be honest about this. I expect everyone to cooperate with the Lafland team. Give them everything they ask for. No stonewalling."

Betsy frowned. "But, Judith, that's like signing our pink slips."

"Not necessarily." Judith pushed her glasses back on her nose. "I'm going to fight this every way I can, but the only chance we have of winning is to be completely honest." Not just because Glenn hated lies and was trained to ferret them out. It was a matter of personal integrity. That was something each member of her team possessed. They might be tempted to deceive Glenn and the other Lafland staff, but Judith didn't believe they would actually do it.

By the time Glenn arrived for their afternoon meeting, Judith had completed the interview schedule. As part of the study, Glenn and his team wanted to interview the IS staff as well as key customers.

"I've booked the Raritan conference room for all of next week," she told him. "The only problem I'm having is getting an electronic whiteboard."

Glenn shrugged, then ran a finger under his collar. It was odd that he had seemed more comfortable in his rented armor than he did in business clothes. Perhaps it was only that the laundry had put too much starch in his shirt.

"We'll make do without one, if we have to," he said. "The important thing is making sure everyone comes to the interviews." He snapped open the locks on his briefcase. "We have a standard pre-interview questionnaire. I know I have it somewhere." He began pulling out papers. "No, not there." He tossed one folder onto the table, then reached back into the briefcase. Judith glanced sideways. One thing she had learned about Glenn Hibbard, in the short time she had known him, was that although he appeared to be organized, his files were anything but.

"Need help?"

Glenn shook his head and continued rummaging. As he did, a brown bag tumbled open.

Judith stared. So that was the important business Glenn had transacted during lunch! He had turned down Tony's invitation, saying he had a previous commitment. Tony undoubtedly thought Glenn was power-lunching. Now Judith knew what he had really done. He had gone out to buy a copy of *Golden Web*! As the color started to rise to her cheeks, she forced herself to think of something, anything else. It didn't work. Every fiber in her body begged to know whether he had started reading it and what he thought of her story. Was he like Tony? Did he think romantic heroines were silly? Or was he like Jonathan Stockton's wife who laughed and cried?

As they settled back to work, Judith found it difficult to keep her attention on Glenn's questions. Why had he bought the book? Oh, she knew he had told Lynette he was going to get a copy, but Judith had thought that he was simply being polite. She had never thought he would do it.

Why? Was it because he found Lynette as attractive as she had found him? Was he still dreaming about that evening the way she was? Judith fumed. If it weren't so patently absurd, she would have said she was jealous.

* * *

Of all the nights for Karen to decide they ought to have dinner together! There were seven days in the week, and she had picked the one when he had important business to take care of. Glenn smiled as he thought about the business. Wouldn't Karen hoot if she knew the reason he wanted to postpone dinner was that Lynette Thomas's book was sitting in his briefcase, just begging to be read?

It was foolish, of course, to assign so much importance to reading a book. After all, it would be waiting for him when he got home from Karen's. Besides, he might not even like it. But Glenn's intuition told him otherwise. If Lynette Thomas had written it, then chances were excellent that he would enjoy it. If nothing else, it would give him yet another clue to the most fascinating woman he had ever met.

Glenn changed into jeans and a sweater, then grabbed the bottle of sparkling juice he'd left chilling.

"Beware of little brothers bearing gifts," Karen said as she accepted the bottle. Karen was dressed as casually as he, her auburn hair pulled back from her face with a large butterfly clip. One curl had tumbled loose, reminding Glenn of the soft curls that had framed Lynette's face. Her hair, of course, was a lighter red, almost blond.

"What kind of predicament do you want me to rescue you from this time?" Karen asked in the tone he had long ago called Sister Superior.

Glenn smiled and dragged one of the stools from under her breakfast bar. "Here I am trying to show you that I've learned the social graces, and you accuse me of ulterior motives. Shame on you, Karen Eldon!"

His sister's raised eyebrow signaled her skepticism. "If you're really into social graces, you can set the table."

"And to think I was so deluded as to believe I was a guest."

"When were you ever a guest?"

"Certainly not Saturday night." Glenn opened a cupboard and removed two plates. "Speaking of which, you owe me."

As she pulled vegetables out of the crisper, Karen gave a theatrical sigh. "I already promised you Broadway tickets. What more do you want?"

"How about an apology on bended knee for that costume? Do you have any idea what it felt like to clank every time I moved?"

She smiled one of those secretive smiles that managed to irritate him as much as her I-know-it-all voice. "Is that the reason you left without so much as a good-bye?"

It was Glenn's turn for a secret smile.

The bantering continued as they prepared dinner, and Glenn had to admit he enjoyed it. As he had told Judith that morning, it had taken a long time before he had considered an older sister more than life's greatest trial, but now that they'd become friends, he realized how much having a sibling meant.

"So tell me the truth." Karen lit the candles. She was serving Chicken Cordon Bleu and had informed

Glenn that candlelight enhanced good food. "Why did you disappear from my party?"

Glenn paused to pour the juice, knowing the delay would annoy Karen. "I did what any knight in shining armor would do. I found a lovely damsel in distress, swept her off her feet, and spent the evening with her." He paused again, watching an expression of incredulity cross his sister's face. "At a diner," he added. "Good food but no candlelight."

Karen laughed. "I never realized you had such a vivid imagination. You ought to consider a career in creative writing."

Glenn raised his glass in a salute. "Odd you should mention that." He clinked his glass to hers. "That's what she does. She writes books."

"Who?"

"The woman I spent Saturday night with."

"Right." Karen drew the syllable out to a long sarcastic exclamation. "And I danced with the Prince of Wales."

"This is me, Karen." Glenn leaned across the table, gesturing with his fork. "When did you last know me to lie?"

Karen exhaled so quickly that the candles flickered as comprehension washed over her face. "You really did meet a woman."

He nodded. "That's where I need your help. She's disappeared."

After Karen agreed to try to find Lynette, she regaled Glenn with stories of her new neighbors.

"Don't you agree?" his sister asked at one point.

He looked at her blankly, suddenly aware he had no idea what she was talking about.

Karen laughed. "You've got a bad case."

"What do you mean?"

She laughed again. "You didn't even hear my last question. Wherever you were, it wasn't in my dining room." Karen laid down her fork and regarded him steadily. "If I didn't know you better, I'd say you were smitten."

Smitten! Absurd! If he had learned one thing from his experience with Michelle, it was that he was never, ever going to feel that way about another woman. No, indeed. Love was a four-letter word that he had deleted from his vocabulary.

Karen was wrong. He had simply had a momentary lapse of attention. It could have happened to anyone. There was no reason to tell Karen that he had been thinking about the last two times he'd sat across a table from a woman. A diner and a coffee shop. A redhead and a brunette. Lynette and Judith. They were as different as two women could be, and yet—try though he might—he could not dismiss either one from his thoughts.

Chapter Six

J udith frowned at the blinking cursor. This was ridiculous. She had never had writer's block, not that
this could truly be classified as that dreaded malady.
Today she had no trouble forming sentences or even
coherent paragraphs. The words were flowing freely.
It was only six A.M., and she had already met her daily
quota of pages. That wasn't the problem.

Charles was. If only he would behave! When she
had outlined *Silver Rose*, she had drawn clear mental
pictures of her hero and heroine. Charles, she knew,
was medium height with dark brown hair and the
warmest of brown eyes. He was dashing and handsome, the perfect hero, except for one thing. He lacked
a sense of humor . . . at least until Marguerite, the heroine, took him in hand.

Why, then, did Judith's fingers insist on typing
words like *auburn hair* and *deep blue eyes*? When did

Charles grow five inches? And how did he suddenly develop a keen sense of humor? It was not only annoying that her hero looked and acted like Glenn Hibbard; it was also absurd and childish. It had to stop.

Judith poured a cup of coffee, then returned to her computer. She would show Charles who was in charge. She instructed the computer to replace every *auburn* with *dark brown*. Blue eyes disappeared with another touch of the keys. As for the unplanned humor, that would have to wait until she returned from work. It was time for another day at the bank with Charles. Judith's hand paused halfway to the power switch. Nonsense! It was *Glenn* she was meeting at the bank!

Women have all the luck, Glenn thought as he hung his suit coat over the back of the chair. They had makeup to camouflage sleepless nights. He, on the other hand, felt as though someone had poured sand under his eyelids and was slowly tightening a steel band around his forehead. Worse yet, he knew he looked every bit as bad as he felt. His eyes were bloodshot and rimmed with dark circles, turning him into the image of a man with a colossal hangover, when all he'd had were two glasses of sparkling juice and two hours of sleep. It was the latter that had wreaked the damage.

Glenn glanced at his watch. Nine o'clock—Judith should be here. One of the things he had learned about her was that she was never late. He opened his briefcase and pulled out the folder on change management.

Yesterday they had reviewed source code policies; today he would learn what progress Judith had made in controlling object code. As he looked at the neatly printed sheets, Glenn realized he had absolutely no interest in computer programs, whether they were in source or object form. All he cared about this morning was whether Lady Emilie Wilshire and Andrew Clayton, the Duke of Bollington, lived happily ever after.

I wonder what Judith would say if I told her I needed the morning off so I could finish reading a Regency romance, he mused. *She'd probably think I was crazy. She'd be right.* A sensible man didn't do things like that, but then a sensible man didn't find himself infatuated with a woman he'd met exactly once.

Glenn walked toward the coffee pot. What he needed was something to bring him back to reality, and that awful-tasting liquid was a good candidate. He pulled a Styrofoam cup from the stack and turned it right side up.

"Stop!"

Glenn turned. "Good morning, Judith." Even to eyes as tired as his, she looked good. Today, instead of pulling her hair back in that knot, it hung to her shoulders. Oh, it was still conservative, a smooth fall of glossy hair, but it looked softer, and she seemed somehow more approachable.

He reached for another cup. "Want some?"

As Judith shook her head, the curls brushed her cheeks. *Nice*, Glenn thought. Then he chided himself for imagining how that silky hair would feel entwined in his fingertips. *Hibbard, you need sleep. You're losing it.*

"I've got a better idea." Judith opened her briefcase and drew out a large Thermos. "Voilà! Real coffee."

It was, Glenn had to admit, a good idea. Undoubtedly they would waste less time than if they went back to Mario's, and yet he couldn't quite suppress the feeling of disappointment. It was only now, when he knew it wasn't going to happen, that he realized he had been looking forward to another hour at the coffee shop. Away from the bank, Judith seemed friendlier and more open, and that, he rationalized, was good for the project. That it also made the morning more enjoyable was something Glenn didn't want to consider.

"Tell me about the people on your staff," Glenn said when he'd emptied his first cup of coffee. One thing was certain: Judith's brew surpassed even Mario's.

It was surely his imagination that she flinched. "If you'd like copies of their personnel files," she said stiffly, "I'll have to call human resources."

Glenn shook his head. "I don't need that kind of information." He had already been given their salary ranges and home addresses, so that he could judge if they were living beyond their means. As far as homes were concerned, no one seemed out of line. Now he needed to know more. Casual conversation had revealed that Judith had taken a trip to England each of the last three years. With the mortgage on her condo, those trips must have stretched her finances. Still, they weren't proof that she was the embezzler. Anyone on the team could be involved.

"I find it makes the interviews go more smoothly," Glenn improvised, "if I know a few personal details about the people."

Though Judith nodded, he saw skepticism in those pretty gray eyes. "They'll all suffer if they lose their jobs," she said.

They wouldn't all lose their jobs unless they were all part of the fraud, but of course Glenn could not tell Judith that. "The recommendation hasn't been written yet," he said. That was the truth, if not the whole truth.

"Betsy's been here the longest," Judith explained. "About five years. She's single, likes jazz and good books."

Though Glenn liked jazz, today books were foremost on his mind. "What kind of books?"

"Almost anything you can name. I've never met anyone who read so many different genres."

"How about you? What do you read?" Probably nonfiction exclusively. He had trouble picturing no-nonsense Judith reading anything light. It had to be his imagination that her eyes clouded. That must have been a trick of the light on her glasses, but it wasn't his imagination that she straightened her spine and moved back a few inches.

"Mysteries and romances," she said almost defiantly. Not at all what he had expected.

Glenn thought of the book that had kept him awake last night. "Do you have a favorite romance author?" Wouldn't it be coincidental if she was a Lynette Thomas fan?

"Diane Roberts." The answer came without hesitation, and Glenn remembered that the bookstore had had a large display of Diane Roberts' books. "She makes the Old West come alive for me."

It was on the tip of Glenn's tongue to ask whether Judith had read *Golden Web*. With a mental shake, he reminded himself that his mission was to uncover a thief, not discuss the book whose characters still lived in his memory, and so he turned the conversation back to Judith's team. "Sam's the one with the tan, right?"

Judith nodded. "He just got back from a two-week honeymoon in Hawaii."

Glenn filed that for future reference. "And Matt? Is he a newlywed, too?"

Judith poured them each another cup of coffee before she answered. "He and Linda have been married for four years. They have two children—Matt, Jr., who's three, and Nicole." Judith took another sip, then raised her gaze to meet his. "They all need their jobs."

"What about you?"

She regarded him steadily, her gray eyes apparently candid. "This job is very important to me."

She hadn't, Glenn reflected, answered his question.

A half-hour delay at the tunnel was just what he didn't need. Now he'd be late for the meeting with the partner-in-charge. Glenn picked up his cell phone, then frowned. A dead zone—another thing he didn't need! He tapped his fingers on the steering wheel. No point in honking the horn like the driver three cars behind him. That wasn't going to accomplish anything other than raised blood pressure. Glenn stared through the windshield as if an angry glare would force traffic to begin moving.

It didn't.

He looked at his briefcase, and a wicked grin lit his face. Why not? He snapped the locks open and reached under the manila folders. A minute later, Glenn was chuckling, the traffic jam forgotten.

'I fear, Milord, you've underestimated your opponent,' he read. Once more Emilie Wilshire had foiled the villain. This time the dastardly Reginald had abducted Emilie, taking her to his ship, completely unaware that it was exactly what Emilie had planned and that soon the victim would become captor.

No wonder Jonathan Stockton had asked Lynette about feisty heroines, Glenn mused. Emilie was quite a woman. As for Lynette, the book only confirmed Glenn's first impression. She was witty, somehow able to make even the most dangerous of scenes seem faintly amusing. What a woman! Though he knew it was nothing more than fascination, he couldn't let Lynette Thomas just vanish from his life.

"Alan was called away," the partner's secretary told Glenn when he finally arrived in Manhattan. "He asked if you could wait."

Glenn smiled as he looked at his watch. There was still time. Though he might not be any closer to discovering the embezzler's identity, there was one thing he just might be able to learn. He started dialing the phone.

"Miss Thomas's editor is Lucy Jankowski," the operator informed him. "Let me transfer you to her extension." But Ms. Jankowski was away from her desk, and the only help her assistant could provide was the name of Lynette's agent. "If you'd like to write her a letter care of us, I'll see that it's forwarded to Ms. Thomas."

A letter? No way. Glenn had poured out his heart on paper once, imploring Michelle to reconsider, to give their love another chance. She hadn't. Instead, she had torn the letter to shreds in front of him, declaring that actions were more valuable than words. Love, she had said, was not the same as being in love.

"Andrea Duncan speaking." Thank goodness the agent answered her own phone! Glenn was tired of talking to intermediaries.

"I met Lynette at a party last weekend," he explained, trying a new tactic. "She dropped one of her earrings in my car, and I wanted to return it to her." Glenn couldn't remember whether she was wearing earrings, but it was the best story he could concoct. "No, I really don't want to mail it." You'd think all these people owned stock in the postal service, the way they promoted it. "Would you give her my number then?"

What was it about Lynette Thomas? Sure, she was beautiful and talented and fascinating, and her book had hit the best-seller list, but was that any reason for her to be guarded more closely than Fort Knox's gold?

"Hi, Andrea. What's up?" Judith's agent rarely called her at the office.

"We've gotten excellent feedback on the Stockton

show," Andrea told her. "Lucy says the phone's been ringing off the hook with bookstores that want you to do autographing sessions and fans who want your address. They're even talking about a second printing."

"That's nice." It was more than nice. It was fantastic news. If she were at home, Judith would be eloquent in expressing her delight, but she wasn't at home. She was in a bank cubicle where sound traveled easily. If she wanted to keep her dual identity secret, Judith could not afford to have her conversations overheard and repeated.

"I got a call, too," Andrea continued. "A man named Glenn Hibbard. He told me a story about meeting you at a party last weekend, something about you leaving an earring in his car. I have to admit he sounded convincing. If I didn't know you better, I might have thought it actually happened."

Judith managed a little laugh. "You know I don't wear earrings."

"Or go to parties."

You're wrong on that one, Judith said silently. *I may not have worn earrings, but I most definitely went to that party.* "I don't think I'll need his number."

"Good girl." Andrea's voice was warm and approving. "You never know about these fans. Some of them are more than a little wacko."

Not Glenn. He's as normal as they come. I'm the one who's crazy.

"What's the matter? Not answering phone calls?"

Judith smiled. "Nice to talk to you, too, Melinda."

She had picked up her voicemail messages, which had included four increasingly irate calls from her friend, but hadn't had time to return them. Being tied up in meetings most of the day had put her behind on her own work.

"You're one popular person," Melinda announced. "I got two calls about you today."

Judith said nothing, knowing that Melinda was only pausing for effect. She started scrolling through her e-mail, checking for urgent messages.

"Karen Eldon called."

There was another significant pause, and this time Judith took the bait. "Do I know a Karen Eldon?"

"You ought to. She was your hostess Saturday night."

That's right. Melinda had said that someone named Karen was holding the party. Judith clicked the "Delete" button, sending the employee club's notice of its annual Radio City outing to the recycling bin.

"Anyway," Melinda continued, "it seems that her brother met you at the party and wants to see you again. She didn't say a lot, but I gather that the guy was impressed."

Judith's hand paused in the midst of dragging a memo from Tony into her archive file. Suddenly the pieces began to fit. In a voice that Judith hoped sounded nonchalant, she said, "I assume Karen told you her brother's name."

"Of course she did. Glenn Hibbard."

So that's who Glenn's Karen was! He had talked about his sister, and he'd spoken of a woman named

Karen, but he had never indicated that they were the same person. Though it was silly to care, Judith couldn't hide her smile.

"Are you going to call him?" Melinda demanded.

"I don't know."

"You're a fool if you don't."

I'm more of a fool if I do, Judith told herself. There was no doubt that Glenn Hibbard was the most attractive man she had met in ages. He was handsome, intelligent, and fun to be with. All that was wonderful. What wasn't so terrific was that he was obviously attracted to Lynette, not Judith.

How do I get myself into these predicaments?

Chapter Seven

"**I**'d like to finish the preliminary risk assessment tonight," Glenn told Judith several days later. "Do you mind working late?"

"Of course not, Simon Legree." Judith smiled as she considered him. "You're even starting to look like an overseer." In truth, he was looking particularly handsome today. Though the dress-for-success books might decree that brown suits were for losers, there was no doubt that on Glenn the brown tweed looked terrific. It was more casual than his usual navy blue or pinstriped suits, a fact that Judith found especially appealing. "Want me to call Mario's?"

Glenn's reply was a short laugh. "Not tonight. What do you think about Francine's?" he asked, referring to one of the most elegant restaurants in the area.

"It sure beats Mario's ham and Swiss sandwiches." Except for the days when Tony insisted on their joining him for lunch in the executive dining room, Judith and Glenn had fallen into the habit of ordering sandwiches from Mario's and eating in the conference room, ostensibly while they worked. In fact, the study was rarely discussed during lunch. Instead, they would talk about music, art, current events, favorite vacation spots, even things as mundane as the weather. The topic didn't matter, at least as far as Judith was concerned. What was important was what they learned about each other. And what Judith had learned was that Glenn was far closer to her ideal man than Andrew, Charles, or any of the other heroes she had invented.

Their conversations were friendly, never going beyond the bounds of professionalism, never verging toward the slightly risqué bantering they had shared in the diner. Judith knew she couldn't expect that. After all, she and Glenn were engaged in a study that would determine the fate of her job and her team's. He had to remain impartial; she could do nothing to influence Glenn. Judith the banker knew that. Judith the woman wished it could be different. And so she agreed to dinner.

Francine's was a small French bistro that did a brisk lunch trade serving onion soup, croques monsieur, and other sandwiches on authentic French bread. At night the lights were dimmed, and the tablecloths changed from red checkered to white linen; the menu became gourmet, and the prices increased accordingly. It was what Melinda called a first date restaurant.

Even if he asked, Judith had no intention of telling

Glenn that she had never come to Francine's for dinner or how infrequent her dates had been. The few she had been on tended to be of the movies and fast food variety. Judith Barlow, it seemed, did not inspire men to romantic gestures on dates. Tonight, of course, was not a date, she reminded herself.

"Your coat, Madame." Though it was the maitre d' who spoke, it was Glenn whose hands touched her shoulders ever so lightly, helping her slide the coat from her arms. It was nothing more than a polite gesture, the act of a man with good manners, and yet the warmth of his fingers lingered, igniting a flame deep within her.

Judith shook her head slightly, reminding herself that they were in the middle of a study. Until that ended, their relationship could be nothing more or less than professional. Lunch and dinner together, casual conversations. Those were permissible. Anything beyond that was not. Those were the rules. The fact that the rules were broken as often as they were obeyed didn't change them or the way Judith felt. Melinda was right; she was conservative, and Glenn . . . Glenn saw her as nothing more than a business associate. It was only Judith with her romantic streak and her compulsion for creating happy endings who was overreacting to a simple touch, wishing the study were over and that Glenn would invite her on a date.

As the formally dressed waiter approached to take their orders, Judith studied the menu. If the food was as good as the surroundings, it would be delicious. From the fresh flowers and silver candlesticks that graced each table to the softly romantic sounds of the grand piano, Francine's provided an elegant dining experience.

"Not quite like the bank's cafeteria," Glenn said with a smile.

Not quite like the diner, either, she thought. How ironic it was to realize that her most romantic evening had been spent in an ordinary diner, while this beautiful restaurant was the scene of a business meeting.

When Glenn's escargots and Judith's pâté were delivered, each eyed the other's dish. "That looks delicious," they said in unison.

Judith grinned. "Miss Manners wouldn't approve, but we could share."

She broke a piece of crusty French bread, spread it with the smooth pâté, then handed it to Glenn. As she reached across the table, her fingers touched his, and once again an electric current shot up her arm.

It's nothing, she told herself. *Sheer proximity and the romantic atmosphere.* Judith knew otherwise. Try though she might, she could not convince herself that what she felt for Glenn was purely professional.

"Can you tell me how the interviews are going?" she asked. Though she wanted to know, Judith asked the question primarily to defuse her tension. It was odd. She wrote about romance, and she hoped that one day she would find a real-life love as wonderful and lasting as those she created for her characters. Though she readily admitted she was a hopeless romantic, she had never expected to find herself attracted to a man who was forbidden to her—at least temporarily.

That was bad enough. Worse yet, Glenn had first met her as Lynette. While he had appeared attracted to the English writer, like every other man she knew, he viewed Judith as nothing more than a friend. It was just her bad luck that she was well on her way to being head over heels in love with him. Not even Judith's active writer's imagination had conjured such a dilemma for one of her characters.

"The interviews are going well." Glenn pried another escargot from its shell and dipped it in the garlic sauce. "I'm learning a lot, including the best places to honeymoon in Hawaii."

Judith raised an eyebrow. Glenn must have worked wonders to get the normally reserved Sam to elaborate on his honeymoon. Both Matt and Betsy had complained that Sam was about as communicative as the horseshoe crabs that littered the Delaware Bay beaches.

"Were you ever married?" Judith regretted the question the instant it was out of her mouth. Glenn's smile froze, and there was no doubt that those deep blue eyes had turned glacial. Why had she been so foolish? Because, Judith admitted, she wanted to know what had caused the sorrow she occasionally saw reflected in his eyes. Because—foolish though it might be—she wanted to know about Glenn the man.

"No." Though it was only one word, the way Glenn said it left no doubt this was a forbidden subject.

Why did I ever mention honeymoons? Glenn asked himself. *I set myself up.* You couldn't blame Judith. Her question was innocent. She had no way of knowing that answering it would dredge up memories he'd sooner forget. Michelle. Jared. That horrible night. *Forget it.* That's what he had to do. Concentrate on the fact that he and Judith were having a pleasant evening and forget everything else.

She looked especially pretty tonight. Though the candlelight reflected on her glasses, when she turned her head ever so slightly, he could see her gray eyes sparkling. She was wearing some kind of perfume, something light and spicy that smelled better than the flowers on the table. And those lips. Right now they were wrapped around an escargot, savoring the flavor. Glenn could think of other uses for her lips, ones that involved savoring of another kind.

Stop it! Where's your sense of professional decorum? It was one thing to have dinner with a business associate, quite another to get involved personally. He was supposed to be totally unbiased when he made his recommendation, and if he couldn't maintain a professional distance, he would have to remove himself from the engagement.

Engagement. Though the word brought back memories he wanted to suppress, it also raised interesting ideas, ones that were very definitely not professional. It was ridiculous. Judith had given no sign that she felt anything more than a professional respect for him. Oh, she was warm and friendly, quite different from the first time he had met her, but her behavior had always been one hundred percent professional. Glenn was the one who was behaving like a teenager.

And so he wrenched his mind back onto safer subjects. "I've drafted the risk assessment," he told Judith. "I'd like to review it with you tonight before I show it to Tony."

She nodded. "No problem, other than that you'd better not tell Tony I saw it first. Even though I'm the point person on the project, he likes to think he's in charge."

"Would I be out of line if I said he seems a strange boss for you?"

Glenn watched Judith's eyes sparkle with amusement. "Not as out of line as I'd be to agree with you."

By the time the waiter brought the check, Glenn was once more laughing. Judith was good for him, no doubt about it. Just being with her helped him banish unpleasant memories. With her dry wit and ready smile, she kept everything in its proper proportion. Judith Barlow was quite a woman.

As he slipped her coat over her shoulders, her hair caught under the collar. Quickly, before she could react, Glenn released the long, thick brown hair, letting his hands linger a moment longer than strict propriety demanded. She felt so good! His fingers brushed the side of her neck, touching skin that was soft and smooth, almost the same texture as the roses that had decorated their table. It took sheer willpower to let his fingers drop to his side. *The study, Hibbard. Remember the study.*

The night was cool and clear with a breeze that tugged leaves from the trees, setting them swirling on the ground. Though it was a night for lovers to stroll in the park, enjoying the crisp fall air, he and Judith were not lovers. Definitely not.

Judith settled back in the car seat and closed her eyes for the briefest of moments. Had she simply imagined it, or had Glenn's fingers lingered on her neck? It had to be her imagination, fueled by the subdued lighting and the romantic atmosphere of the restaurant. For although he had been friendly since the beginning of the project, there had been nothing in Glenn's demeanor to suggest that he viewed her as anything more than a client. The man was professionalism personified. It was only Judith whose romantically inclined imagination imbued the simplest of gestures with a significance he had never meant.

When they returned to the office, Judith did her best to concentrate on the risk assessment. She must have made coherent comments, for Glenn gave her no puzzled looks. But Judith's mind was not focused on the papers in front of her. Instead, it replayed the touch of Glenn's fingers on hers as they passed a piece of bread and the gentle caress of his hand as he helped her with her coat. He was sitting only three feet from her, separated by a conference table. Three feet, and yet it could have been a continent. All he saw was Judith Barlow, DDA project leader. Judith Barlow, woman, was invisible. The fact that it had to be that way was no consolation, absolutely none at all.

It was after eleven when Glenn rose. "Let's call it a night."

"Sounds good to me." Judith wasn't sure how much longer she could have endured sitting so near him.

Somehow, it wasn't a problem during the day. Then she could be totally professional. Perhaps it was the dinner they'd shared. Perhaps it was the knowledge that they were the only people on the floor. All Judith knew was that the last few hours had been sheer agony.

As they stepped out of the conference room, Judith switched off the light and started toward the elevators.

"Judith."

She turned.

Afterward she was not certain who made the first move. All she knew was that she found herself in Glenn's arms, and suddenly his lips were on hers. They were firm and smooth and sweeter than any dessert she had ever tasted. They touched, cajoled, and promised her delights beyond any she'd ever dreamt. For a moment she thought of nothing but how right it felt to be here, to have his arms hold her close, to feel his heart beat next to hers. And in that moment Judith knew she had lied to Jonathan Stockton. She wanted both her fantasies and her dreams to come true. For an instant she had found them.

Glenn had no idea how long they stood there. It could have been a second; it could have been a lifetime. All he knew was that nothing had ever felt so good. Judith fit into his arms as if she belonged there, and those lips . . . ah, yes, those lips. They tasted better than anything he had dreamed, with a sweetness more powerful than the strongest drug. One taste and he was hooked.

There was a clank and a whir as the elevator began to move. Though it was one of the most difficult things Glenn had ever done, he dropped his arms and stepped back a pace.

"I shouldn't have done that," he said. "It's against all the rules." Professional and personal. If he had learned only one thing from his experience with Michelle, it was that he would never again let himself care about a woman, for caring was the first step toward heartbreak.

Glenn slipped off his shoes and wriggled his toes. More than taking off his tie or hanging up his suit coat, removing his shoes signaled the end of the work day. It was Friday night, and though he had a full day of work ahead of him tomorrow, tonight he would try his best to put work behind him.

Work had been a lot easier in California. But in California there had been no attractive brunette with sparkling gray eyes to change an ordinary assignment into something special and to make him almost sorry when the day ended. Although he had always enjoyed his job, it had never been like this. Now he actually hummed—albeit tunelessly—while he shaved and showered, and rather than pondering the points he would delve into that day, he found himself thinking about Judith, wondering what new things he would learn about her. For each day taught him more about Judith Barlow than it did about the operations at Sixth National.

Part of him was discouraged by the fact that he had

found no clues to the embezzler. It could be anyone on Judith's team or no one, for there was always the outside possibility that the thief was not one of the support staff. The other part of him was elated by the fact that nothing pointed to Judith. Though he had no proof, Glenn's intuition told him she was as honest as he—more so, for she hadn't come to the bank under false pretenses.

As for the kiss they had shared, the less he thought about that, the better. Dreaming about that was as silly as his fantasies about Lynette.

Glenn padded into the kitchen and dished out a bowl of chili. While it and the cornmeal muffins were warming in the microwave, he scanned the television schedule. It was ridiculous. He had already studied it, assuring himself there were no new Jonathan Stockton specials and that promising young author Lynette Thomas was not appearing on any of the other talk shows. He had even called the local cable stations to be certain their listings were correct. Lynette Thomas had disappeared from the airwaves as thoroughly as she had from his life. If it hadn't been for her book and the videotape he had made, Glenn would have thought he had imagined her.

He glanced at the book still lying on the coffee table. He had read it twice, a record for him. Not only was this the first time he had read a romance, it was also the first time he could remember rereading any book, except textbooks, of course. To his surprise he had found himself so captivated by the people in the story that he hadn't wanted the book to end. When it had, he'd started it again.

It was like the tape. He had played that so often that he could practically recite the interview. Though he'd watched it dozens of times, Jonathan Stockton remained nothing more than a television celebrity, while Glenn could almost swear he knew Lynette far better than one evening at a diner and a twenty-minute TV segment would warrant. Such was the power of the human imagination.

Glenn reached for the VCR control, then shook his head. It was time to return to reality. *Face it, Hibbard. Lynette was a nice dream, the kind of fantasy every man has once in his life. Beautiful and unattainable. What you had was a chance meeting, like sitting next to a movie star on a transcontinental flight. It made a nice memory, a good story to tell your buddies, but it wasn't reality.*

He continued his internal monologue as he grabbed a glass. Lynette might have seemed like the perfect woman, the person Glenn had dreamed about ever since he was a child. She might be the person he had wanted Michelle to be, but he would never know for sure. Lynette hadn't returned his calls, though he had done his best to reach her. He couldn't find her. Now his only choice was to put the memory aside along with her book and the tape and go on with his life.

For once Glenn took his own advice.

Chapter Eight

"Certainly, Herb. I'll be right over." Judith blocked the next hour on her electronic calendar. That way if Tony or anyone on her team wanted to find her, they would know she was in Herb Carlton's office. As the senior vice president of commercial banking, Herb was considered the owner of the DDA system and Judith's primary internal customer. Though they both attended the monthly steering committee meetings, it was unusual for Herb to call Judith, and she wondered why he had asked for the meeting. Perhaps he wanted to discuss the implications of the system's possible outsourcing.

"We've got a challenge," Herb said as Judith took a chair in front of his polished cherrywood desk and opened her portfolio. Herb was a middle-aged man of medium height with medium brown hair and medium brown eyes. There was nothing about him that warranted a second look until he smiled. Then his face seemed to come alive. The fact that he was smiling now told Judith the challenge was a positive one. "Excelsior Manufacturing," Herb said, referring to the bank's largest customer, "has agreed to the loan terms we proposed. In return, we're going to sweep their DDA accounts into a higher interest account."

Judith scribbled a few notes on her pad as she considered Herb's statement. Though the request sounded simple, she knew that it would require a modification to the most complicated program in the system.

"How soon?" she asked. As she told her team, while nothing was impossible, some things were expensive and took a long time to accomplish.

Herb leaned back, the smile fading from his face. "I promised we'd have it ready by the November cycle."

Trying not to cringe, Judith nodded. The November cycle for Excelsior would be run the Saturday of Thanksgiving weekend. Though she had no special plans for the holiday, she was sure Matt and Sam did, and Betsy had hinted that she wanted to fly to Aruba for the weekend.

"Can you do it, Judith?" While Herb might phrase it as a question, Judith knew there was only one possible answer.

She nodded. The timing was awful. Even if they had had no other projects underway, the timing would have been challenging. As it was, she and the rest of the team were preoccupied with the outsourcing study. That consumed valuable hours of every day. Still, she might be able to turn Herb's request to the team's advantage.

"What do we tell the consultants?" Matt asked when Judith described the project. "They said they were going to shadow us next week." Shadowing was the consultants' term for spending the entire day with a team member, recording everything he did.

Judith smiled. "Let them shadow you. Maybe when they see just how complex that code is and how very good you guys are, they'll realize that it makes no sense to outsource DDA."

For the first time since Glenn Hibbard had appeared at the bank, Judith saw genuine smiles on her team members' faces.

"You're working too hard." Judith looked at Tony in surprise. Oh, she wasn't disputing the facts. Between the outsourcing study, the new system requirement, and her writing deadline, she hadn't had much time to sleep, and each day it became more difficult to camouflage the dark circles under her eyes. The surprise was that Tony had noticed her fatigue. It was not like him to summon her to his office merely to discuss her work habits, particularly when she was working long hours.

Judith shrugged. "It's an occupational hazard." Doubled. No doubt about it, trying to juggle two full-time careers was more difficult than she had anticipated. But of course, Tony would never know that.

He leaned forward, his most earnest expression pasted on his face. "It's obvious you know how critical this study is," he said, tapping his pen on the desk. "There's a lot riding on it." In addition to Judith's promotion, the rumor mill hinted that Tony was angling for advancement of his own. Senior vice president had such a nice sound, not to mention the extra stock options it brought. But if DDA were outsourced, not only would Judith not get her promotion, but it was also likely that Tony—since his responsibilities would be diminished—would not qualify for his coveted new title.

"I don't think you'll have any trouble with Hibbard," Tony continued. He tapped more slowly now. It was one of his more annoying habits, like calling his stockbroker while Judith was in his office. To keep herself from grabbing the pen from him, Judith looked out the window. Though most of the leaves had fallen, the pear tree's mahogany-colored foliage provided a vivid contrast against the blue sky.

"You seem to be handling the study pretty well."

"We've made a lot of progress," she agreed. Why couldn't Tony admit the reason the study was going well was that she had put years of solid hard work into making the bank's DDA system the best in the state? It wasn't chance that was making the Lafland partner happy with Glenn's reports.

"Of course," Tony said. It was the way he said it, not the simple words that annoyed Judith. "I'm just concerned about the new project for Herb Carlton. Are you sure your team has got that under control?"

Judith nodded. As Tony continued to tap his pen, Judith realized that he seemed nervous. That wasn't like Tony. Perhaps he was more concerned than she had realized about his promotion. "You've seen the schedule," she said in a voice that was designed to be reassuring. "It's aggressive, but we'll meet it."

Laying down his pen, Tony made a point of studying a sheet of paper on his desk. It was, Judith saw, her project schedule. "You're going to start final testing the week before Thanksgiving?"

Again she nodded, thankful that the tapping had stopped. "We'll test that Thursday and Friday. I don't expect any problems, but the worst-case scenario has us working all that weekend."

Tony brightened. He liked words like "scenario." "Are you comfortable with your team's progress?"

"Of course."

There was a moment of silence when Judith was afraid he would reach for the pen again. Instead, Tony picked a folder off his desk, glanced from it to Judith, then laid it back down. "Good," he said. "That's the reason I wanted to talk to you. I was supposed to attend the EBA conference in Atlanta this month." The Eastern Bankers Association met twice a year, and their conferences were among Tony's favorite perks. Since they were normally held in resort areas, he frequently scheduled a long weekend in conjunction with the meeting, thus affording himself an inexpensive vacation.

"I had planned to go." He leafed through the contents of the manila folder. "Even had all the reservations made. Then I discovered there's an important fund raiser that Thursday night. It's one I can't afford to miss, so I thought maybe you'd go to Atlanta in my place." Tony raised his eyes to Judith's. His were mildly questioning, and she wondered if he saw excitement reflected in hers. Not even in her wildest dreams could Judith have imagined Tony offering her a trip to Atlanta for the one weekend of the year that she most wanted to be there.

"As long as the study and Herb's project are progressing well," Tony continued, "there's no reason you can't be out of the office for three days."

Judith was tempted, so tempted. Yes, she could use the break. Yes, the EBA conference was supposed to be a good one. But there was more.

"It'll be good for your career," Tony said.

"I'm sure it would be." Tony might think he knew everything, but he did not know that the reason she wanted to attend the conference had nothing to do with Judith Barlow's career at Sixth National. It had everything to do with Lynette Thomas and her books.

For the past month Judith's agent had been urging her to participate in a large autographing party, arguing that it would be a way to capitalize on the publicity from the Stockton show. At the time that she had heard about the signing session, Judith thought it sheer bad luck that it was being held in Atlanta the Friday and Saturday following the EBA conference. Not just in Atlanta but at the same hotel. Knowing that Tony normally extended his stay, Judith had refused to participate in the writers' party. It was far too risky. Though she'd be dressed as Lynette, there was no sense in tempting Fate and possibly being recognized. Now there was no reason not to go.

"You'll have a great time," Andrea said when Judith told her of her change of plans.

"I expect to." There was no denying the bubble of excitement that welled up inside her at the thought of being Lynette again. Putting on a strawberry blond wig and the green contact lenses was more than playing dress-up. It was acting out a fantasy, and each time she did it, Judith found she enjoyed it more. She knew it wasn't reality, but for a few hours it felt good to put aside sober Judith Barlow, to forget that she was a conservative banker. Being Lynette was fun.

"I don't think it should interfere with anything we're doing," Judith said as she told Glenn about her trip to Atlanta. "After all, it's only three days."

He looked at the schedule spread in front of them and nodded slowly. "I'll be spending most of that week in Manhattan, anyway. We've just landed another major client, and Alan wants me to attend some of the preliminary meetings with him."

Judith smiled, though she seethed inwardly, as she had each time she'd been alone with Glenn since that night at Francine's. The man was infuriating. Though it had been a week since they'd had dinner together, a week since he'd kissed her so tenderly, he had made absolutely no reference to it. It was as though the evening had never happened. Glenn was as polite as ever, and they bantered as they had before they'd gone to Francine's, but never once—not in words or even by a glance—had he acknowledged that they had shared a moment that was more than professional. How could he forget it so easily when the memory of that kiss and all it had promised kept Judith awake at night?

Judith had tried exorcising the memory by writing it into *Silver Rose*, but even after Charles and Marguerite had shared the sweetest of kisses and Marguerite had spent sleepless nights wondering whether Charles cared for her or was still fascinated by the Lady Louise, Judith had been unable to relegate the memory to its proper place in the back of her subconscious.

Glenn, it appeared, had no such problem.

In all his thirty-one years, Glenn had never met a woman as maddening as Judith Barlow. She was beautiful, intelligent, utterly desirable, and supremely exasperating. It had been seven days, twelve hours, and thirty-six minutes since he had held her in his arms. They had worked together for five of those seven days, spending at least six hours a day in each other's company, and yet not once had she given him the slightest sign that she remembered how they'd clung together, their lips expressing the desire their eyes had reflected all evening.

Though he tried valiantly to deny it, for Glenn it had been the single sweetest thing that had happened to him in years. For Judith it had obviously been an eminently forgettable interlude. She was once again totally professional, treating him with the same courtesy she had shown him before, never once crossing that invisible line between professional and personal demeanor, never once intimating that they had shared anything more than a meal together. He'd waited for her to make the first move, to give him some indication she wanted to talk about it, but she hadn't.

In his more rational moments, Glenn had told himself that was good. They needed to remain on a purely professional footing. His less than rational moments made him wonder why women found him so easy to forget. Michelle, Lynette, and now Judith. It was enough to make a man doubt himself, and if he already had doubts . . .

It wasn't as though he wanted a permanent relationship. Certainly not. "Relationship" might not be a four-letter word, but it bordered on the 'L' one. Glenn didn't want that. No, indeed. But he did want Judith to acknowledge that something had happened that night. Instead, he got silence. It was annoying and irritating, but he'd just found the way to end it.

Flipping open the yellow pages, Glenn dialed the first travel agent in the book. "I need reservations for Atlanta."

"Some people have all the luck." It was Matt who spoke, a wry smile creasing his face. When Judith's team met for their daily status briefing, she had told them of her impending trip to Atlanta. Though she had kept her voice neutral, Glenn had noticed her gray eyes sparkling with anticipation. He doubted that the others had seen the glint of pleasure, but then he doubted the others studied Judith Barlow as carefully as he did.

Ever since the team had started working on the special request for Excelsior, Judith had invited Glenn to join the daily meeting. It was, he suspected, an act designed to demonstrate how efficiently her team worked. Had the objective of his study been outsourcing, Glenn would have been impressed. Judith's team was as good as she claimed, and he doubted an outsourcer could do their work better or cheaper. But since Glenn's mission was to discover who had tampered with the DDA programs, he refused to let himself be swayed by the group's obvious technical expertise. It was exactly that expertise that had enabled one of them to divert money into his or her private account.

"It's not just Judith who's lucky," Sam said, crooking a smile at Betsy. "Someone—I wouldn't want to mention any names—was spotted driving one very fancy brand-new green Jaguar this morning."

Betsy flushed. "You're just jealous, Sam."

"You're right about that. So, what did you do—rob a bank?"

My question precisely. Though he kept his expression impassive, Glenn watched Betsy flush again. Unlike Judith's, this did not appear to be a flush of pleasure but one of embarrassment. Unless he was greatly mistaken, Betsy had something to hide.

"Did you ever hear of the lottery?" Matt asked. "Maybe Betsy had the winning numbers last week."

"Or maybe she has one humungous twenty-year car

loan," Judith suggested. "Now if we could get back to Herb Carlton's request . . ."

Though the team seemed to dismiss Betsy's new car as nothing extraordinary, Glenn was not convinced that it was so innocent. He had noticed Betsy's expensive jewelry. It was possible the pieces were gifts, but the comments he'd overheard told him she had bought them for herself over the past couple months. Jewelry and a new car on Betsy's salary? Not likely. Betsy Gordon had just moved to the top of Glenn's suspect list.

"Any chance of a ride in that new car of yours?" Glenn asked her later that day. "I've always wanted a Jag."

Betsy's smile radiated pure pleasure. "Me, too. It's a dream come true."

And how had she paid for that dream? Glenn made a note to check the bank's loan files. If Betsy had indeed taken out a car loan, she had probably done it at Sixth National, where she had the advantage of lower employee rates.

"I'd be glad to take you for a spin, but not tonight." Though she continued to smile, her eyes refused to meet his. "I've got to be somewhere right after work." It wasn't his imagination that she was uncomfortable telling him that. Glenn's antennae vibrated again. He'd have to find out where she was going.

A light rain was falling by the time they left the office. Glenn had checked the files and learned that not only had Betsy not taken a Sixth National loan, but she also hadn't borrowed money from any other bank. Somehow Betsy Gordon had paid cash for an expensive automobile. It was up to him to find out whether that cash had come from illegal sources.

"At least let me see the Jag up close and personal," Glenn said as he walked to the parking lot with Betsy. She grinned, and this time he could detect no nervousness.

The car was beautiful. Glenn couldn't deny that any more than he could deny that he wished she were driving a junker and wearing costume jewelry. It didn't matter what he wanted. The fact was, Betsy was a suspect. Glenn slid behind the wheel of his car, ready to follow her. But as Betsy gunned the engine and her tires squealed on the wet pavement, he could only close his eyes in horror.

"I do love you. How many times do I have to tell you that?" Michelle's blue eyes sparkled with tears. "You just won't listen."

"Oh, I'm listening." Glenn balled his fists to keep from slamming them against the wall of his hillside home. In the distance the sun was setting over the ocean, turning the Pacific from blue-gray to red. Sunset lingered only a few moments. The pain of Michelle's words would last forever. He unclenched his hands, forcing himself not to touch the woman he loved. "What I heard was that you plan to marry my best friend."

"I thought you'd understand."

"Oh, sure." Though his sarcasm made her flinch, Glenn couldn't stop himself. "I understand that you and Jared played me for a fool. You pretended you

loved me. You even wore my ring. And then when Jared came around, you forgot about all those promises you made."

A single tear slid down Michelle's cheek. *"We didn't plan it. We didn't want to hurt you."*

"But you did. That's the bottom line. You and my best friend betrayed me!" And how that hurt. Glenn and Jared had been friends since college. Glenn had watched Jared make a disastrous marriage and suffer through the inevitable divorce. When he'd suggested Jared move to California and had helped his buddy find a job, he hadn't expected that Jared would steal his fiancée. The possibility had never, ever occurred to him. Glenn and Michelle were engaged. Glenn and Jared were good friends.

Oh, he had known Jared and Michelle were spending time together. Fool that he was, he had encouraged it. When he had spent six weeks in Chicago on a special assignment, he had asked Jared to make sure Michelle wasn't lonely. Friend that he was, Jared had done that. Unfortunately, he had done more. Much more. He and Michelle had fallen in love.

"Get out of here!" Glenn shouted at Michelle. *"I don't ever want to see you again!"*

He hadn't. Though no one was sure exactly what had happened, Michelle had lost control of her car on the drive home, plunging into a steep ravine. By the time the paramedics had reached her, there was no need for first aid. Michelle was dead. Glenn's anger had killed the only woman he had ever loved.

Chapter Nine

Thanksgiving had come to the Peachlands Hotel. There were signs of it everywhere, but none more so than in the grand ballroom. Today, instead of snowy white linen, the tables were draped in harvest green with centerpieces of bronze chrysanthemums and dried gourds spilling from cornucopias. It was a room designed to foster thoughts of Pilgrims and blessings, and it might have worked for Judith if only she hadn't been so bored.

The conference was dull. No, she amended, it was far worse than that. She searched her brain for another adjective, one that would describe the utter tedium she had endured for the past day and a half. It wasn't just that the speakers were pompous, so impressed with their own presence on the podium that they seemed to forget their primary purpose, which was to provide some basic edification for the audience. She could ignore that and the tasteless jokes targeted at the eighty percent male audience. But the fact that she had found conversation with the other attendees equally boring was something she could not ignore.

Was it, she wondered, the fault of the conference, or had she created the problem? Did all the people seem dull simply because she compared them to Glenn Hibbard? Were the jokes feeble only because she remembered his sharp wit? Melinda was right. She had reached the dangerous stage when she started measuring everyone by one man.

Judith glanced at the back of her name tag for the number of her luncheon table and made her way through the crowd, looking at the numbered placards protruding from the top of the centerpieces. Though this was a time-honored way to identify tables, it was enough to make a florist cringe.

"Great conference, isn't it?" a man asked as he took the seat next to her.

Judith hoped her smile looked sincere. What was great was that in twenty-four hours it would be over. Then she'd go back to her room, slip on the curly reddish blond wig and the green contact lenses, and for two days she would become Lynette Thomas. If only she could survive until then.

As her pager began to vibrate, Judith felt a frisson of fear. She had talked to Tony and the team earlier that morning, and everything had been under control. Since everyone knew she checked her voicemail regularly, there was no reason for a page unless there was an emergency. Fleeting images of Melinda in a car accident flashed through Judith's mind in the second before she saw the area code.

"Want to play hooky?" a familiar voice asked as the call went through.

"Glenn!" Judith grinned as relief flooded through her. No emergency. "Where are you?"

"Probably about three hundred yards from you." Glenn's voice was warm with amusement and something else, something she had never heard and was afraid to identify. "I'm in the lobby. Meet me there?"

Judith flew toward the escalator. It didn't make sense. Glenn was supposed to be tied up in meetings with his new client for the rest of the week. Why, then, was he in Atlanta? The answer that flitted through her head was so wonderful she hesitated to even think it.

"What are you doing here?" she demanded when she saw him. Her eyes moved slowly from the top of his auburn hair to the tip of his shoes, reassuring herself that he was not a figment of her imagination, someone she'd conjured up to alleviate the boredom of the conference.

Glenn's blue eyes sparkled with mirth as he smiled at her, treating her to the same careful assessment she'd just given him. "You look terrific," he said without answering her question. "I like your hair that way."

Instead of her usual smooth coiffure, she had curled her hair. This morning Judith had had doubts about the new image. Now, seeing the expression on Glenn's face, she had none. The approval in his eyes was worth the effort with the curling iron.

"Why are you in Atlanta?" she repeated.

As if for an answer, Glenn placed his hand on the back of her waist and guided her toward one of the couches. "Do you want the official story or the truth?"

Judith's eyes widened in surprise. "You mean to say there's a difference? I think I'd better sit down."

Although there were few people in the lobby at this hour, Judith noticed that Glenn had chosen a secluded corner. It was a wise precaution, since neither of them could afford rumors that the study had been anything other than impartial. That made Glenn's trip to Atlanta all the more puzzling.

Glenn sat facing her, and his grin broadened. "There sure is a difference. I told Alan we had some outstanding questions that couldn't be resolved over the phone."

"But there aren't any open issues. Are there?"

Glenn feigned dudgeon. "You doubt my word? Of course there are open issues." The smile he gave Judith made her thankful she wasn't attached to a heart monitor. With the way hers was pounding, she would surely have triggered an alarm. "It's just that the issues are not bank-related," Glenn continued. "What I couldn't resolve over the phone was the fact that I wanted to spend the day with you."

Judith was sure her face would crack. No one should smile this much. It stretched the skin and caused wrinkles, and she couldn't have cared less. For the first time in her life Judith believed in the existence of a fairy godmother. How else could her wishes have been answered? Glenn was here, rescuing her from the conference, and he'd said he wanted to be with her. Her, not Lynette.

Keep it cool, Judith. Don't rush it.

"I don't believe this," she said with a soft laugh. "The man who told me he never lies just told his boss a big one." And the man who had never seen her as anything other than a client—except for that one night at Francine's—was now looking at her the way he did at Lynette.

Glenn smiled with a tenderness that wreaked more damage on her heart, this time causing it to skip a beat. "You know what?" he asked. "I have new respect for my sister. She told me a white lie wouldn't hurt one bit, and she was right. C'mon now," he said, rising to his feet. "Let's get started on this hooky."

Moments later, Judith was back in the lobby carrying a small bag with the items Glenn had said she would need.

"First stop is Egypt," he announced as they walked through the revolving doors. Though it was November, the day was unusually warm, and shoppers crowded the large mall that adjoined the hotel. While they waited for the valet to bring the car, Judith blinked, as much from Glenn's announcement of their destination as from the sunshine.

"Egypt?" Since it appeared that ordinary rules were suspended today, Judith wouldn't have been surprised if Glenn had chartered the Concorde to take them to Cairo for dinner.

"The Georgian version." He qualified his statement as he helped Judith into the car. She settled back and let herself enjoy the ride. There was no doubt that it felt good to be away from the convention, and even less doubt that it was wonderful to be with Glenn. Judith wasn't sure what had wrought the change in him, why he was suddenly willing to be more than business associates, but at the moment she had no intention of asking. Melinda might call it cowardice, but Judith knew it was prudence. What woman in her right mind would risk spoiling what promised to be a perfect afternoon with the man of her dreams? Not Judith Barlow, that was for certain.

Glenn swung the car into an underground garage and switched off the ignition. "Is this Egypt?" she asked, pretending to study the white lines on the ground and the few cars that were parked on this level. "You should have told me to pack my imagination as well as my bathing suit and a dinner dress."

"Trust me."

"The last time I heard that line, it was delivered by a man who wanted to sell me a used car."

"And I'll bet you bought it."

"You'd lose the bet. Now, where's the Nile?"

Fifteen minutes later Judith's eyes widened in surprise, for in front of her was a scene worthy of the most romantic book she'd ever read . . . or written. While many hotels boasted an indoor swimming pool, Glenn's hotel went beyond that, creating a fantasyland. Palm trees, sand dunes, and a blazing sun set the mood that a scaled-down Sphinx and three pyramids completed. It was, as Glenn had promised, Egypt in Atlanta. The pool itself, long and undulating, looked so much like the pictures Judith had seen of the Nile that she hesitated to enter it. After all, weren't the Nile crocodiles notorious? Though it was completely irrational, the sight of a quartet of white-haired matrons frolicking in one of the river's bends did little to allay Judith's concerns. A healthy imagination was not always a blessing.

The hesitation Judith felt as she shed her beach jacket had a far different cause. Suddenly Egyptian crocodiles with a penchant for dining on tourists' toes seemed positively benign. Glenn Hibbard, on the other hand, sent a frisson of apprehension down her spine.

Melinda was right. She was a coward. It was one thing to face Glenn when she had the armor of her perfectly tailored suits, and quite another when she was clad in a bathing suit.

Two teenage boys whistled. Glenn merely smiled. "Cleopatra would have had you killed," he said softly. "I hear she had no qualms about eliminating the competition."

The man was perfect! His words warmed Judith even more than his frankly appraising glance had done. Somehow he'd managed to say exactly the right thing, telling Judith he found her attractive without a hint of crudeness.

"Let's swim." Maybe the water would cool the heat that suddenly suffused her body. They swam side by side, matching each other's strokes, and though they exchanged no words, Judith was vividly aware of Glenn's nearness. After they'd swum the length of the Nile several times, Judith pulled herself onto the bank.

"Do you need these all the time?" Glenn touched the glasses she'd put on as soon as she'd climbed out of the pool.

"Afraid so." It wasn't just that she was near-sighted. The glasses were also part of her costume, one of the things that differentiated her from Lynette Thomas. Since the phone calls had stopped, Judith had no way of knowing whether Glenn still thought about the English author, but she had absolutely no intention of doing anything to remind him of her. Today was Judith Barlow's day, and no one—not even Lynette—was going to spoil it.

She sank onto the sand and leaned back against one of the pyramids. "I feel like I'm a million miles away from the bank."

"That's how you're supposed to feel when you play hooky." Glenn's eyes were serious as he took one of Judith's hands in his. For a moment he looked at her palm; then he began to trace the lines with his index finger.

"Are you a palm reader?" It was the simplest of touches, and yet it was strangely exciting, sending fiery sensations to every nerve ending in her body.

"I only wish I were and that I could read the future." He drew her hand to his lips, pressing a soft kiss onto the palm. Judith's pulse began to race. Nothing she had read—or written—had prepared her for the sweetness of Glenn's caress. No wonder ladies of old extended their hands for kisses!

"I took a chance coming here," Glenn said. "I wasn't sure you'd be glad to see me, especially since the study isn't over." His eyes met Judith's, and she could read the uncertainty in them, an uncertainty she found all the more appealing because it mirrored her own. "It's been difficult for me," Glenn continued, "pretending you were nothing more than a client, even pretending I didn't remember our dinner at Francine's."

As the four women walked by, they smiled, and Judith heard one whisper loudly to another, "I do declare, there's nothing like young love, is there, Edith?"

Judith wasn't sure about young love, but she was certain there was nothing like the way she felt today. Happiness coursed through her veins. Though she could feel herself blushing, Judith kept her eyes fixed on Glenn. "I thought you were sorry about that night, and that's why you never mentioned it."

Glenn's laugh was short and derisive. "I thought *you* regretted our kiss." He took both of her hands in his. "We know how we're supposed to feel and act: impartial, professional, no personal involvement. I can quote you chapter and verse of the ethics manual." The cynical note in Glenn's voice left no doubt of his opinion of that particular manual. "The problem is, that's not the way I feel. You're not just a client to me, Judith."

"I stopped seeing you as an adversary a long time ago," she admitted.

His smile matched hers as he put his arm around her shoulders and drew her close to him. "For today we're just Judith and Glenn, playing hooky from everything else."

It was a magical afternoon, more wonderful than anything Judith had experienced. They swam and lounged, talking about everything and nothing, simply enjoying the freedom to be themselves.

At length Glenn looked at the sundial standing in the corner of the room. "I made dinner reservations."

"In Paris?" It wouldn't have surprised Judith to learn Glenn had found a restaurant that captured the Parisian atmosphere as completely as the hotel had Egypt.

"Sorry to disappoint you." Glenn chuckled. "I thought we'd eat in Georgia." And he would say no more.

As they drove along the winding road to the restaurant, Judith smiled. They were in Georgia, all right, but it looked more like the antebellum South than anything she'd seen in the early twenty-first century. Huge live oaks bordered the lane, their branches forming a canopy, and at the end of the mile-long drive was a mansion straight out of *Gone With the Wind*. Judith looked down at the wine-colored dress she'd chosen and frowned. Surely she should have worn a hoop skirt and caught her hair in a snood. As though he could read her thoughts, Glenn squeezed her hand. "You look beautiful."

If she'd been asked what they ate for dinner, Judith could not have answered. Yet she could have described in intimate detail the scent of Glenn's aftershave, the warmth his hand sent through her as he brushed her arm, the taste of peach nectar on his lips. Though she knew they must have spoken, she could remember nothing their lips had said, for their eyes were expressing thoughts neither of them was ready to put into words.

The moon was high, the stars twinkled overhead, and if she hadn't known it was unlikely, Judith would have said there were magnolias blooming as they left the restaurant. She looked at Glenn for a long moment, then nodded as he slipped his arm around her waist and drew her closer to him.

Slowly, as though they had all the time in the world, they walked along the lane. The oaks formed a protective arch over them, and when the road wound out of sight of the mansion, Glenn turned toward Judith. Here there was little light, for the trees blocked the moon, but Judith did not need brilliant illumination to see the tenderness in Glenn's eyes. As he drew her into his arms and lowered his lips to hers, her lips curved upward. This was where she wanted to be.

Judith was a skilled writer, a woman whose prose could make people laugh and cry. Her book had won accolades for the emotions it conveyed, and readers had told her that she had somehow managed to put into words their innermost feelings and longings. Yet Judith's imagination had not prepared her for the reality of kissing Glenn in such a romantic setting.

It was magic, pure magic.

Chapter Ten

With a sigh of frustration, Glenn reached for the remote control and switched on the TV. Maybe if he concentrated on the world news, he could forget about the woman who had haunted his dreams last night.

"Give the gift of love," a comely woman exhorted the viewing audience as she held out a flacon of perfume. Glenn punched the channel advance button. The last thing he needed to think about were gifts of love. The day he and Judith had spent together had been wonderful, no doubt about it. But love? Glenn wasn't sure any such thing existed.

A talk show. That would be less dangerous. At this time of the year, the guests were likely to be accountants advocating year-end tax planning or economists predicting the stock market's cycles for the coming year. Boring but predictable. Glenn's eyes widened. A woman in a hoop skirt reminiscent of *Gone With the*

Wind stood next to the show's host. No tax planning there. She was probably a representative of the Chamber of Commerce, touting the local attractions.

"We're delighted to announce a very special guest at our extravaganza tonight," she said in the most delightful Southern drawl Glenn had ever heard. He wasn't remotely interested in whatever type of extravaganza she was hyping, but her voice kept him from advancing the channel. He leaned back on the pillows and listened. "Tonight we'll have with us the author of *Golden Web*, Miss Lynette Thomas."

For a second the words did not register. When they did, Glenn grabbed the pen and notepad the hotel had so conveniently provided. Peachtree Romance Writers. Peachlands Hotel. Autographing party. Tonight, six to nine.

For the first time, Glenn believed in Fate. He had promised himself that he would see Lynette again, if only to prove she wasn't as fascinating as he had remembered. So far all his efforts had been in vain. Now he had a second chance. Fate had brought him to Atlanta at the same time as the woman he wanted to see. His eyes sparkled with anticipation as he picked up the phone.

"You have three new messages." Judith frowned at the mechanical voice's greeting. Her frown deepened as she listened to Matt's increasingly worried voice. Thank goodness the calls had been made last night after Judith would normally have stopped taking messages. At least now she didn't have to explain why she hadn't checked her voicemail yesterday afternoon. The simple fact was, she hadn't thought about voice-mail, e-mail, or anything else related to work. For a few hours, she had played hooky so completely that she had almost forgotten she had a job. Now she was back to reality.

"You could have paged me," Judith told Matt when he answered the phone. "But thanks for letting me enjoy my dinner." She hoped her voice didn't betray just how much she had enjoyed that dinner. "What's wrong?" Matt's messages said only that there was a problem, not its nature. Judith flipped to a clean sheet of paper and prepared to take notes.

"The regression test failed." Matt's voice resonated with frustration. "Even allowing for the changes to Excelsior's accounts, the calculations don't match. I think it's something in the rounding."

Judith's eyes narrowed as she began to doodle. Re-gression testing was the last step before putting a mod-ified program into production. Once programmers were satisfied that a change worked properly, they ran one final test, using data that had been developed spe-cifically for the purpose. This last test was designed to prove that the modification didn't inadvertently cause a problem somewhere else in the system. It was very rare that the results of the modified code failed to match the expected ones.

"Are you sure you're using the right set of data?" she asked. Though it was unlikely, if Matt had been working late, he might have pulled test cases that didn't match the predicted output.

His exasperated sigh told Judith the answer even before he said, "Sam and I double-checked that." Judith could hear Matt tapping something against the desk, a habit he had when he was worried. Idly, she wondered if Tony's annoying phone calls were also contagious. "I don't understand it," Matt said. "I *know* my code is good."

As Judith yanked the drapes open, sunlight streamed into the room. It was a beautiful morning in Atlanta, or it would be if she could help Matt. "You're the best, Matt," she said. They weren't idle words. Matt was good, and if he was having a problem, something was very wrong. "Why don't you e-mail me a copy of the code, and I'll look at it. Maybe I can spot what's wrong."

Judith phoned for room service. At the rate she was going, she would barely get to the conference in time for the final luncheon. Matt's e-mail message arrived along with her oatmeal and orange juice.

An hour later Judith was as mystified as Matt, and as frustrated. She could find nothing wrong with Matt's program. If only she hadn't agreed to attend the autographing sessions tonight and tomorrow, she could skip the rest of the conference and fly back to Newark. Judith was certain that if she worked with the team, they would be able to find the error. But she couldn't back out of the book signings at this point without disappointing her publisher, not to mention the Peachtree Romance Writers, who had promoted her book so diligently.

"I really hate to do this," Judith told Matt when she

had finished reviewing the program, "but we need to get Tony involved. He's been away from the code for a few years, but I'm willing to bet he still remembers that program." Judith drained the last of her coffee and wished she had ordered a second pot.

"No go."

"What do you mean?" Even if he was rusty, Tony was their best chance of finding the problem.

Matt had resumed his tapping. "I just talked to Tony's wife. He's got the flu so bad he can't even get out of bed."

Judith groaned. This was the proverbial case of being between a rock and a hard place. Thank goodness she had built extra time into the schedule. It would be tighter than she liked, but the odds were good they would still be able to get the modified program into production for Excelsior's November cycle.

"Don't bother Tony, then. I'm flying back Saturday night." She had deliberately scheduled a late flight, even though the second autographing session ended at five, so that she could spend extra time with the Peachtree writers. "I'll plan to meet you in the office Sunday morning," she told Matt. "Ten o'clock okay?"

"Sure thing."

As she started to dry her hair, Judith reflected that, for more reasons than one, this was going to be a memorable weekend. It had started early and well with Glenn's unexpected visit. How it would end was still unknown, although Judith forced herself to remain optimistic. There had to be a simple reason the rounding calculations did not match.

What wasn't simple was how she felt about Glenn. Yesterday had been wonderful. For the first time in her life, Judith had felt that a man saw her as a woman, not just a friend. She had reveled in Glenn's attention and that oh-so-heady feeling that he found her attractive. But when she had awakened this morning, she had been beset by two fears that, try though she might, she could not dismiss. The first was that no matter how attracted Glenn might be to her, he preferred Lynette. And the second was that he would be angry when he learned she and Lynette were the same person.

Judith couldn't ignore the memory of Glenn explaining his deep-seated dislike of deception. There was no question of glossing over the fact that she had deliberately concealed something important from him. The only question was how he would react. Though she knew many more things about Glenn than she had twenty-four hours earlier, this was one area where Judith knew nothing. It was not a comforting thought.

Glenn scowled at the red light, then glanced at the store on the right. Mistletoe and holly. Bah, humbug! It was too early to hang Christmas decorations. Next thing he knew, they'd be playing carols. As the light turned green, he pressed his foot toward the floor. A block later, he stomped the brake. Christmas carols. Bah, humbug! He felt like Scrooge. All because of that television show.

That wasn't fair, and Glenn knew it. The problem wasn't the show. It wasn't even the fact that Lynette was going to be in Atlanta tonight. The problem was

Glenn himself. Unfortunately, identifying the cause of the problem didn't make resolving it any easier. He ought to be on that plane heading back to Newark right now. If he had any brains, any common sense, any decency, he'd be doing exactly that. Instead he was sitting in traffic cursing himself and counting the hours until he'd see Lynette again.

And to think he had blamed Michelle for being attracted to Jared! Poetic justice, irony—call it what you may. The simple fact was that he was no better than Michelle.

There was no rational explanation. With the way he felt about Judith, he shouldn't be able to think about another woman, much less concoct a web of lies so that he would be able to see the other woman. But he had. Glenn Hibbard, the man who claimed he hated deceit, was now a class-A liar. What a fool he was!

"So why are y'all nervous?" Melinda asked in her best Southern drawl.

It was an hour before the Friday evening autographing session was to start, and Judith, finding herself with an unexpected case of jitters, had called her friend. Though she tried to tell herself that her nervousness was caused by worries over the failed regression test, Judith knew that was only a part—a small part—of the reason a host of butterflies had taken up residence in her stomach. As she looked across the room and saw the sea-foam green dress and the curly reddish blond wig reflected in the mirror, Judith rolled her eyes. Melinda could be matter-of-fact about it because she wasn't the one who had to act out the charade.

"I can't imagine why I'm nervous," Judith said lightly. "Maybe it has something to do with pretending to be someone I'm not." She took a deep breath, trying to quiet the butterflies or at least—as the facilitator in her assertiveness class had said—to get them to march in formation.

"But," Melinda pointed out in a voice that was maddeningly logical, "you are Lynette Thomas. She's just a different part of you."

The theory might be good, but the butterflies weren't buying it any more than they bought the deep breaths. Judith rose and began to pace the length of the room.

"You know I'm worried about someone recognizing me. I met a lot of people at this conference, and some of them might be staying for the weekend."

Judith could almost hear Melinda wave her hand, dismissing the thought. "What are the chances of one of them attending your autographing party?"

About the same as the odds of Lynette's knight in shining armor heading Judith's outsourcing study. Incredibly long odds, and yet it had happened. As she considered the probability of something so unlikely happening a second time, Judith started to relax. At least she didn't have to worry about Glenn. He was in New Jersey, hundreds of miles away. Thank goodness. If he had stayed, Judith would have been hard pressed to explain her absence during the two autographing sessions.

"You'll be fine," Melinda told her. "I know you will."

Judith was not convinced.

Glenn pulled the end of the tie through the knot and adjusted it carefully. He brushed his hair, then stared at his reflection. It was ridiculous. He hadn't been this concerned about his appearance since he'd been a teenager on his first date. Now he was a grown man, meeting a woman who had made it clear she didn't care to see him again, and he was just as nervous as he'd been fifteen years ago.

Lynette might not even recall their evening together. Glenn frowned. That was a possibility he didn't want to consider. After all, what man wants to think he's so easily forgotten? But as the weeks had passed and she hadn't returned his calls, Glenn had realized it was not only possible, it was likely. *I can deal with that*, he assured himself, straightening his shoulders and holding his head high. What was important was to see Lynette once more, to exorcise her memory and then go on with life. He owed that much to Judith.

But as he walked the short block to the Peachlands, Glenn's thoughts were not of a lovely banker. Instead, he remembered Lynette's strawberry curls, those incredible green eyes, and the softness of her British accent.

Soon, he told himself. *Soon*.

Judith took a deep breath as she entered the Peachlands' grand ballroom for the second time that day.

The room had been transformed since she'd eaten lunch there. Tonight there were small tables around the perimeter, each bearing two stacks of books. A few larger tables, laden with trays of food and bowls of punch, were placed closer to the center. There were, however, no chairs except those allotted to the authors, for the goal was to have readers mingle with their favorite authors, moving from one table to another, and if all went according to plan, buying many more books than they would ordinarily consider.

Judith's hostess, Rebecca, introduced her to several other writers, then whisked her to the table they'd be sharing. "I hear the roar of fans out there," Rebecca said, gesturing toward the main doors. She straightened the tall conical headdress that was part of her medieval costume. "Why is it I think of lions in the colosseum?"

As the doors began to open, Judith smiled. For a while at least, she could forget the day's problems. Tony's flu and the DDA test would disappear while she was Lynette Thomas, and tonight she wouldn't worry about Glenn and his fascination with Lynette. It worked. For the next half hour Judith had little time to do more than smile at fans, exchange a few sentences with each, and sign their copies of *Golden Web*. It was exhausting, exhilarating, and, as she confided to Rebecca, more than a little intimidating. "They look at me like I'm someone special. Don't they understand that I'm just like them?" Judith clipped her words. Tonight she was Lynette, and that meant an English accent.

Rebecca shook her head. "It's called fame. You'll get used to it."

There were, Judith discovered, a surprising number of men at the signing. Though almost all of them asked for the books to be addressed to their wives, Rebecca hinted that many of them were the actual readers. "They pretend," she whispered as she bent down to pull another supply of books from the carton beneath the table, "but we know they read them, too."

So Glenn wasn't as unique as he had feared. Someday when she told him the truth about Lynette, Judith would tell him how many men had come to the Peachlands to buy romances. If she were lucky, he would laugh.

Though the room was overly warm, filled with scents of perfumes that should never have been mixed and hundreds of conversations that reminded Judith of lions' roars, it was the friendliest crowd she had ever experienced. The fans didn't seem to mind waiting for a chance to talk to an author and take home an autographed copy of a romance.

Judith smiled at the next woman in line as she answered her questions about Jonathan Stockton. "He's even more charming in person than he seems on TV, if you can believe that," she said. "There's something about him that makes every woman feel she's queen for a day." He was almost as good at that as Glenn. But Judith didn't want to think of Glenn exercising his charm on every woman he met the way Jonathan Stockton did. What made yesterday so special was that the magic had been for her alone.

Judith glanced a few yards behind the woman, and as she did, her words froze in mid-sentence. It couldn't be. It was her imagination; that's all. She had been thinking of Glenn. That was the only reason she believed he had just entered the ballroom. But as the tall auburn-haired man moved through the crowd, Judith knew it was not her imagination. No one else walked with that particular gait. No one else had hair that shade of red. No one else stared at her with that intensity.

Oh, no! Glenn was supposed to be hundreds of miles away at a meeting with his boss. Why was he here? Judith gripped her pen so tightly that the ridges cut into her fingers. What a ridiculous question. There was only one reason Glenn was here tonight, and that was to see Lynette. The irony of the situation did not escape Judith. Was it less than an hour since she'd thought her problems had been put on hold? Now she had a new worry. Perhaps the real reason for Glenn's trip to Atlanta had been Lynette. Perhaps his day with Judith had been nothing more than a diversion while he waited for the main event.

Though it was more difficult than she would have believed, Judith fixed a smile on her face and turned her attention back to the woman in front of her. Maybe if she wished very hard, Glenn would disappear. He did not.

"Will you save me from a fate worse than death?" he asked in the mellow voice she knew so well.

At her side Rebecca snickered. Judith refused to make eye contact with her tablemate. She needed all her wits to deal with Glenn. The way to survive this, she decided, was to play her role to the hilt. She would be Lynette, nothing more, nothing less. When the evening ended, Glenn would vanish from Lynette's life for the last time. It was a great strategy. Unfortunately, he wasn't making it easy.

Judith raised one eyebrow and answered in her best British accent, "Just what fate would that be?"

"Being the only person in this room without an autographed copy of your book."

As Rebecca snickered again, Judith raised one brow in what she hoped was a regal look, slightly haughty and definitely not overly friendly. The last thing she wanted to do was encourage Glenn.

"That's one wish I can certainly grant." Judith opened a copy of *Web* to the title page. "How would you like it addressed?"

As she began to write, her eyes widened in shock.

A fate worse than death. The words echoed in Glenn's head as he entered the grand ballroom, and though he tried to dismiss them, he could not. It was odd. He hadn't thought of that phrase in weeks, and now he couldn't forget it. It must have been the memory of the first time he had met Lynette and the prospect of seeing her again that triggered the memory.

"Good evening, Lynette."

She looked up, and for the briefest of instants he would have sworn she recognized him. Then, although a smile remained on her face, it was the same one he'd seen her give every other person in line. Cordial but not overly friendly. A professional smile. He wanted more. And so he said the first words that came into his mind, the ones that had formed the silent refrain.

Again, he saw a flicker of recognition before she was able to suppress it. She knew who he was, but for some reason—probably the same one that kept her from returning his phone calls—she wasn't going to admit it, at least not voluntarily. She obviously hoped he would take the book and leave. She was wrong. If Lynette thought he was going to simply disappear without an explanation, she had reckoned without the Hibbard stubborn streak. He hadn't waited in that endless line surrounded by chattering women just to be brushed aside. He wanted something—even if only the admission that she remembered the night at the diner—from her.

As Lynette began the inscription, Glenn's gaze moved from her beautiful face to her hands. There was something familiar about those long, slender fingers with their delicately tinted nails and the ornate cameo ring.

The ring.

Glenn's eyes narrowed, and a cold certainty swept through him. He had seen that ring before.

"I can't wait to meet Lynette Thomas," he heard the woman behind him say to a companion.

But she's not Lynette, he wanted to tell the stranger. *She's an impostor.* It couldn't be coincidence. Glenn was a man who depended on logic and facts, not blind emotion or intuition. Logic told him the ring was unique, and that even if there were a second copy, the odds of its appearing in Atlanta the same day Judith Barlow was wearing hers were extremely slim.

Suddenly the pieces to the puzzle slid into place. It was an odd picture, one he had never expected, and yet there was a perverse logic to it. The ring was Judith's, and unless he was greatly mistaken, she and Lynette Thomas were the same person.

It was preposterous. Or was it?

"Remember me?" he asked as Lynette handed him the book.

Her face was paler than before, but her green eyes met his with what appeared to be candor. "Should I?" she asked. Judith had gray eyes and wore glasses. Her hair was light brown, not red. On the surface, the two women didn't look alike, and yet . . .

Should she recognize him? Yes, indeed! Glenn nodded. "We met at a costume party. I was a knight in armor." *I'm also the principal consultant at your bank, although I doubt you'll admit that.*

Lynette—or was it Judith?—paused for a second, her head tilted slightly to one side as though she were considering his words. "Oh, yes." Was it only his imagination that the British accent sounded assumed? "We ate at a diner, didn't we?"

And at Mario's and Francine's and last night at the plantation. But of course she wouldn't admit to those meals any more than she would admit she was Judith Barlow. Glenn made an effort to keep his voice as calm as hers. "I've been trying to reach you since then," he said.

The author who shared the table with Lynette

looked at him, her brown eyes assessing. "There are other fans waiting," she said firmly. Glenn shook his head. He would leave when he was ready, when Lynette answered his question.

This time Lynette lowered her eyes, apparently unwilling to meet his gaze. Perhaps she found lying difficult. "Actually," she confessed with a faint smile, "I had a book deadline and couldn't spare the time to ring up anyone."

It was an unusual choice of words. Oh, Glenn knew the English spoke of ringing someone rather than phoning them, but he suspected it was more of a Freudian slip. She had to realize he'd seen the ring. She had been careful not to wear it to that Halloween party, and he knew she hadn't had it on the Stockton show, for Jonathan Stockton had discussed her ringless fingers when he asked her about the men in her life. But tonight for some reason she had worn it. Had she forgotten, or was it simply that she hadn't expected anyone who knew Judith Barlow to be here?

Glenn could feel the anger begin to seethe deep inside him. How could she be so cool? She was a terrific writer, but she had missed her calling, for she was an even better actress.

"I'm anxious to read your book," Glenn said, ignoring the fact that he'd already read it twice. "I'm hoping to learn something about you." That was not a lie. Though he thought he knew Judith well, he had been wrong. Now he would have to reevaluate everything he knew about her.

When she had signed the book, Glenn moved to the

other side of the room and leaned against one of the columns. Narrowing his eyes, he considered the woman in the green dress. The hair was a wig, and she must be wearing colored contact lenses. As he watched her autographing books and smiling at the seemingly endless stream of fans, Glenn wondered how he had missed the similarities. The smile was the same one he had seen every day at the bank. The little gesture with the left hand was one he had noticed Judith making. No wonder Lynette had seemed so familiar to him when he watched the videotape. At the time, he had thought it was simply because he had played the tape so often. Now he knew there was another reason. The woman was familiar because he spent the better part of each day with her.

No wonder he had been reminded of Judith when he had watched the Stockton show. When it had happened, he had blamed it on random associations. In truth, it had been far from random. His subconscious had made the connection immediately. The rest of his mind had not been so quick.

Judith was Lynette. Lynette was Judith. Why? That was what Glenn didn't understand. Why had Judith gone to such lengths to keep her writing a secret? Being a best-selling author was nothing to be ashamed of. Most people would flaunt their success. Why hadn't she?

As he recalled Jonathan Stockton's questions about the book's cover, Glenn thought he understood Judith's reluctance. More than most banks, Sixth National was stodgy. Hadn't Judith told him that the rumor mill could kill a career? If the powers that be at the bank learned that one of their employees wrote romances, there might be censure.

That still didn't explain why she hadn't confided in him. She knew he was trying to reach Lynette. After all, he had called half the people in the Manhattan phone book trying to find the elusive author. At least one of them must have given her the message. But still, she hadn't told him she was Lynette. Why not? There was only reason Glenn could imagine: Judith did not trust him.

Why did that thought hurt so much?

Chapter Eleven

"**I** want to hear all about Jonathan Stockton," Rebecca announced as she bit into her oversized hamburger. The two women had ordered sandwiches delivered to Judith's suite after the autographing party and were reveling in the opportunity to talk, unencumbered by their costumes or lines of fans. "I suppose you know every author tonight was jealous because you were on Stockton's show instead of her."

"But, Rebecca, you've been on the *Today Show* half a dozen times." Rebecca was the author of fifteen historical romances whose astronomical sales had caught the attention of the media as well as contributing nicely to her publisher's bottom line.

"Yeah," Rebecca agreed, "but let's face it. There's no one like Jonathan. Those eyes, that hair, that voice . . ." She let her own voice trail off before she took a sip of peach-flavored ice tea.

Judith laughed, remembering. "The only thing I thought about was how I was going to keep from throwing up all over his gorgeous suit."

"Nerves! Aren't they great?" It was Rebecca's turn to laugh. "Every time I think I'm over them, they strike again."

Tonight it wasn't nerves that bothered Judith; it was the question of why Glenn had come to the autographing party and whether, once he had arrived, he had recognized her ring. How could she have been so careless as to wear it? Judith had known a moment of pure panic when she had seen the ring. After the magical day she and Glenn had spent together, she had realized she would have to tell him about her alter ego if they were to have any hope of a future together. But until the study was over, Judith had not wanted anyone to know about her writing. Too much was at stake. Her job, those of her team, her own fragile ego.

There had been no doubt that Glenn had been attracted to Lynette at the diner, but when the calls had stopped, Judith had hoped he'd forgotten the English author. It appeared he had not. Glenn was still infatuated with Lynette, and plain Judith couldn't compete.

"Tell me the truth." Rebecca's words brought Judith back to reality. "Was Jonathan Stockton right? Is there a special man in your life?"

Judith shook her head slowly. Twenty-four hours ago she would have disagreed, for then there had been a special man—a very special man—in her life. Tonight there was none. A look of concern flashed across Rebecca's expressive face. "I'm sorry," she said simply. "I don't know what I'd do without John. He's not just my husband; he's my best fan, and he's always there when I need encouragement. That helps so much."

To cover her wistfulness, Judith took a long sip of tea. As she had told Jonathan Stockton, her dreams included a man like the one Rebecca described. For a few hours she thought she'd found him. She was wrong.

Wild animals paced their cages. Grown men did not. Unfortunately, simply knowing he shouldn't be wearing a path in the hotel's thick carpeting didn't stop Glenn's feet. He was an adult. He should not, absolutely should not, be behaving this way. She was only one woman, and there were plenty of other women in the world. Glenn tried his best to ignore the voice that told him there was only one Judith and that he'd waited over thirty years to find her.

He switched on the TV and forced himself to sit on the straight-backed desk chair. There, he'd managed it. His feet had stopped moving. His thoughts, however, were not so easy to control.

Had she deliberately set out to make a fool of him, or had it happened inadvertently? No matter what her motives, the result had been the same. He'd been left feeling ridiculous, dreaming about a woman who didn't exist, who was no more than a wig and a pair of contact lenses. A fool! That's what he was.

If he had hoped the eleven o'clock news would focus his attention on something other than Judith Barlow and her perfidy, he was mistaken. The first segment highlighted the Peachtree Romance Writers' autographing extravaganza. There she was, smiling that remote smile that stopped one step short of being provocative. Glenn punched the power button. The last thing he needed was another reminder of Judith Barlow, Lynette Thomas, or whoever she was pretending to be tonight. What he needed was ...

A wry grin split Glenn's face. Revenge was such an ugly word. He wouldn't use it. Instead, he preferred to say that Judith would soon learn this was a game two could play.

Judith was almost ready for bed when she heard a firm knocking on the door. "A package, miss." The bellman handed her a large cardboard box bearing a florist's logo. Bemused, Judith wondered who had sent the flowers. No card on the outside. Perhaps the florist had put it inside so it wouldn't be lost. But as she slipped the ribbon from the box and drew off the cover, she found no card, only six perfect camellias. Judith sighed with pleasure. Someone had obviously read *Golden Web* and knew that the heroine's favorite flowers were camellias. But who? A call to the front desk revealed that the card hadn't been dropped there, and the florist's staff had only a record of the sale, not the name of the purchaser.

Someone was thoughtful, romantic, extravagant, and wanted to remain anonymous. Who? As Judith closed her eyes, she pictured Glenn's face. She shook her head. Anonymity was not Glenn's style. He had made no secret of his desire to contact Lynette after their evening at the diner, and Judith knew from her dealings with him at the bank that he was normally direct. If he had sent Lynette the flowers, he would have signed his name.

Judith placed the camellias in the small refrigerator and climbed into bed.

It was the strangest alarm she'd ever heard. There were no harsh sounds, no buzzing or clanging. It almost sounded like music. Judith buried her head more deeply in the pillow. The noise continued. It had to be a dream, for now she imagined she heard a voice singing. Absurd. She was more tired than she had thought if she was imagining singing in the middle of the night. The song continued. As the words began to penetrate her consciousness, Judith's eyes flew open. Incredible. She knew those words better than anyone in the world. It was no dream, nor was it an alarm. Instead, a man was outside her hotel door serenading her with the same song Andrew Clayton, the Duke of Bollington, had used to woo Lady Emilie Wilshire.

Judith bolted out of bed and grabbed her robe. A quick look through the peephole revealed what she had expected. A tall, dark-haired man properly dressed in formal Regency clothes stood outside her doorway. He carried a flute, probably the closest thing he could find to Andrew's flageolet, as he sang the ode that had won Emilie's heart.

The digital clock glowed bright red: 3:04. Why on earth was anyone awake, much less singing, at such a ridiculous time? As Judith opened the door and prepared to demand exactly that of the unknown musician, she started to laugh. It had been three in the morning when Andrew had stood underneath Emilie's window, trying to convince her of his love. In *Golden Web* Emilie had been receptive to the musical courtship, believing it highly romantic. Judith found it highly disruptive and vowed that she'd never again interrupt her heroine's sleep in the name of love.

"Very nice." Though her words were polite, her tone was one of dismissal. The man continued to croon, as though he were unaware of her presence. If it hadn't been the middle of the night, she might have found the serenade appealing. But it *was* the middle of the night, and the only thing Judith found appealing was the prospect of uninterrupted slumber.

"You've made your point. Why don't you go home now? You'll only waken the other guests."

It was as if she had not spoken. When Judith started to close the door, the man blocked it with his foot. And still he did not miss a beat.

"What do you want?"

The refrain that had taken her days to compose was her only answer.

"Go home!" she hissed. "You're making a spectacle of me." Several other guests had opened their doors and were peering into the corridor.

As the refrain came to an end, the man bowed low in front of her. "Your servant, milady," he said, sweeping the floor with his hand. He had style; she'd grant him that. Unfortunately, right now she didn't want style; she wanted his departure.

"Who paid you?" she demanded.

The man's face was a parody of guilelessness. "Surely you would not mock your faithful servant's devotion." Though Judith could see a faint glimmer of amusement in his eyes, his words betrayed no humor. The man was a professional, no doubt about it.

"Why are you here?" This was the most ridiculous conversation she'd ever had. Who would have thought she would be standing in her bathrobe interrogating a man whose only crime was to serenade her in the middle of the night?

"Your mistrust wounds me greatly," he replied smoothly. "I sing out of love for you."

As he raised the flute to his lips, Judith groaned. Not another chorus. Andrew had sung for half an hour before Emilie capitulated. Surely this man would not remain that long. Surely the hotel management would insist that he leave. He shifted his weight slightly as he fingered the instrument, and Judith seized the opportunity. Slamming the door shut, she double-locked it. Whoever he was, he could sing in solitude. She was going to sleep.

But sleep eluded her, and so she paced the living room of her suite, trying to guess who was responsible for the flowers and the minstrel. Though Judith's agent or Melinda might have sent the flowers, Judith knew neither of them would have hired a minstrel. It could be an anonymous fan. That was possible, though unlikely. There was only one other suspect: Glenn.

Ah, yes, Glenn. The flowers were a considerate, romantic gesture, like the restaurant he had chosen for last night's dinner with Judith. The serenade was precisely the offbeat humor that he had shown Lynette that first night at the diner. A man who greeted a woman with quips about a fate worse than death would think nothing of causing her to be serenaded when all she wanted was a long, uninterrupted sleep. The only thing that seemed out of character was Glenn's anonymity. The Glenn she knew—the Glenn she *thought* she knew, Judith corrected herself— would not have hidden his identity.

She clenched her fist. What a fool she had been, thinking Glenn would be attracted to her. Judith, the real Judith, wasn't pretty enough or interesting enough to hold his attention. She might love Glenn—and Judith was afraid she did—but she couldn't go through life playing a role. She needed to be loved for herself. Unfortunately, Glenn seemed to prefer Lynette.

"Hello, again." Glenn's lips turned upward in that smile Judith knew so well. It was almost a replay of the previous evening. The authors were back in the grand ballroom, which still bore its festive decor. The fans had come, and so had Glenn Hibbard. The primary difference was that this afternoon the historical authors had agreed to wear ordinary street clothing rather than their costumes.

"Good afternoon." Judith had donned an English accent along with her wig and colored contact lenses, being careful to leave the cameo ring in her room. Last night had been a close call. Fortunately, it appeared Glenn hadn't noticed the ring, or, if he had, he hadn't connected it with Judith. For if Glenn, the man who hated deception, had realized that Judith Barlow and Lynette Thomas were the same woman, he would have erupted with fury.

"Did you want a second book?" She tried to smile, though her stomach was tied in knots. This was what she had feared. Glenn cared little for Judith. He had come to Atlanta to see Lynette, for only a deeply infatuated man would brave the crowds of fans to see an author a second time. Judith pulled a book from the stack and opened it, her hand poised to write. "Perhaps for your sister?"

Too late she realized what she'd said. Though Glenn had told Judith about his sister, she couldn't remember whether he'd mentioned her to Lynette.

"What makes you think I have a sister?"

Bad move, Barlow. He knows he didn't tell Lynette about Karen.

"It's the story all the men use," she said in the lightest voice she could manage.

"I see." Glenn's blue eyes were piercing, making Judith wonder just what it was he saw. Of course he didn't see that, behind the wig and the contacts was Judith Barlow, the woman he had courted so tenderly forty-eight hours earlier. He wouldn't look so calm if he did.

"You're not wearing my flowers." Was it her imagination, or was there a hint of pain in his voice? Surely not, and yet if he cared deeply for Lynette, he might be disappointed.

"Flowers?" His question confirmed that the camellias were his. Judith felt a surge of annoyance. He hadn't sent a card with them, yet he acted as though she would know he had ordered them. "Which ones were yours?"

From the way his lips tightened, Judith knew she had hit a sensitive nerve. Good! He had certainly touched her most painful places. The nudge Rebecca gave Judith said she had noticed Glenn's return and would want to know all about Judith's persistent fan as soon as the autographing session ended.

"Pink roses."

He was testing her, but Judith was ready. Two could play this game. She raised one eyebrow. "Perhaps the front desk misplaced them. I don't recall any pink roses. White, yellow, and red, but no pink."

The woman behind Glenn began to move impatiently. "I'm sorry, sir," Judith said in a voice that betrayed no sorrow. "If you're not going to buy a book, I'll have to ask you to step aside."

He leaned forward until his face was only inches from Judith's. "I don't want a second book," he said. "What I'd like is a second chance."

As lines went, it was a good one. Judith, the author, resolved to file it away for the next time one of her fictional heroes needed to persuade the heroine. Judith, the woman, wondered why she found it so difficult to refuse Glenn. She wanted to. Oh, yes, she did. But she said only, "I beg your pardon."

"Will you have dinner with me tonight?"

"Go ahead," Rebecca urged her.

"Yes, go ahead," the woman behind Glenn chimed in. "Give the rest of us a chance to get a book."

For a second Judith hesitated. Dinner meant continuing the charade, pretending to be Lynette, trying to remember what Glenn had told Lynette and what only Judith knew. It would be awful. She ought to refuse. She would refuse. And yet how could she, when this might be her only chance to discover exactly why Glenn had come to Atlanta and who it was that he loved?

Slowly she nodded.

The first burst of fiery anger had subsided, leaving white-hot embers that needed little more than a light breeze to fan them into flames once again. Fortunately tonight there would be no cause for anger. Tonight two rational adults would share a perfectly civilized dinner, during the course of which one would unmask the other.

Glenn had no doubt about the outcome of the evening, for he had planned each step with the precision that made him so successful as a consultant. He knew how to achieve his goal. Glenn had always operated under the premise that prior planning prevents poor performance, and so nothing was left to chance.

It was a foolproof plan; by the end of the evening, she would have told him the truth.

She was sure he had chosen it deliberately. The revolving rooftop restaurant was as different from a small diner in New Jersey as could be. Here there were no pea-green Formica booths with clashing blue Naugahyde seats. The tables were covered with impeccably laundered white linen, and the chairs would not have looked out of place at Versailles. It was the perfect restaurant, a setting so idyllic a romance writer would have been forgiven for incorporating it into her next book. Why, then, did Judith long for a slightly overweight waitress with aching feet and a plastic name tag? Why did she wish the string quartet with its soft music could be replaced by a dilapidated jukebox blaring a Springsteen song? Why was she deluding herself, thinking that if she could relive that night at the diner she would tell Glenn that Lynette Thomas was a pseudonym? It was foolish, for no matter how hard she wished it, they could not go back in time.

They were seated at one of the prime tables where they had an unobstructed view of the Atlanta skyline. It was, Judith had to admit, a spectacular sight. Darkness had fallen, and now the city sparkled with lights that seemed to rival the stars. If Glenn had brought her here as Judith, she would have been enchanted. As it was, she seethed inwardly at the knowledge that only two days ago he had been romancing her, and now he was with Lynette.

Afraid that her anger would be revealed if she looked at Glenn, Judith gazed into the distance, pretending she was trying to identify the landmarks.

"I heard this was one of the finest restaurants in the area." Judith conquered her anger long enough to look at him as he said, "I thought maybe if I took you someplace nicer than a diner, you might not disappear when the evening's over."

You're wrong about that. I most certainly shall vanish after today. As soon as you answer my questions, I'll be—as the teenagers say—history.

Judith smiled, reminding herself to use Lynette's English accent. "The diner had nothing to do with it. I enjoyed that night." More than she would ever admit, for that was when she had started to fall in love.

"But you did disappear," he countered. "You were like Cinderella, only you forgot to leave me your shoe."

"It would have been difficult to walk with only one."

"I offered to carry you."

"You did more than that, as I recall."

As their waiter approached, Glenn shook his head slightly, and the man stopped at another table.

"There I was playing Ivanhoe," Glenn said, his blue eyes sparkling with apparent mirth, "and you accused me of being Rhett Butler."

"A slight from which you've undoubtedly recovered."

"Alas, fair lady, the wounds fester. They need your healing touch."

It was madness to be bantering like this, as though they were back in the diner. Too much had happened since that night to let them return to that simple camaraderie with its honest attraction, and yet Judith could not suppress the memories. She had enjoyed that night immensely, and so, it appeared, had Glenn.

He leaned across the table, covering her hand with his. "Has anyone told you that you're beautiful when you blush?" He lifted her hand to his lips and pressed a kiss on the back. "You're the most beautiful woman I've ever met."

The spell was broken. His voice was the epitome of sincerity, his words the ones every woman longs to hear. Every woman. That was the problem, for Judith had heard Glenn say virtually the same thing two days earlier. She had believed him then. Now she knew the man was a superb actor, capable of feigning deep emotions. All he needed was scriptwriter to provide a few new lines.

She laughed lightly. "I'll bet you say that to all the women you meet."

His hand caressed hers ever so slightly, and his eyes seemed guileless when they met hers. "You're much too modest, Lynette. It's the truth, not idle flattery."

Why had she agreed to come tonight? This was supposed to be her opportunity to unmask Glenn, to learn whether he loved her or still harbored his fascination with Lynette. It wasn't supposed to be such a painful experience, where everything he said or did reminded her of their day together and how she'd been fool enough to believe he loved Judith. This wasn't going the way she'd planned it.

Mercifully the waiter brought their drinks, and Glenn relinquished her hand. He leaned forward, his expression faintly puzzled. "You know, I still can't believe how green your eyes are. They're almost unreal."

Somehow she managed to swallow the drink without choking. It was an innocent comment. It had to be. "My eyes are the same shade my mother's were." That was true; they had both had gray eyes.

"I can't help comparing tonight to that meal we shared in the diner," Glenn continued. "Doesn't it feel good to be out of costume and not playing a role?"

It was a perfectly logical question, given the circumstances, yet there was something about the look he gave her that told Judith there was more to Glenn's question than the words themselves. First that quip about her eyes, and now this. It was almost as though he were probing, seeking something. But what? Had he recognized the ring after all? Was he expecting her to reveal her identity? For a second Judith was tempted until she reminded herself of the study. If Glenn hadn't guessed—and she still believed he would have confronted her directly rather than trying to trick her into an admission—she did not want to jeopardize her position at the bank.

"You never did tell me why you were in Atlanta," Judith said when one waiter had whisked their menus away and another delivered a basket of freshly baked rolls. "Are you here on a business trip?"

Glenn placed a pat of butter on his bread plate before he replied. "No business." His eyes met hers with a look of utter guilelessness. "The only reason I came to Atlanta was to see you."

It wasn't going the way he planned. He had thought the romantic atmosphere would remind her of their dinner at the plantation, and that she would finally admit Judith and Lynette were the same person. She hadn't. She sat there as cold as an icicle, pretending she was nothing more than an English author he'd met once before. Cool and calm, she reminded Glenn of the ice maiden he had met his first day at the bank. Judith had thawed; this woman had not. He had tried compliments, thinking they would mellow her. They hadn't. If anything, she had seemed hostile when he had told her she was beautiful. Women! Did anyone understand them?

His next tactic had been a few barbed comments, a couple double entendres. He had thought those would anger her enough that she would slip and reveal herself. They hadn't. The woman was tougher than he'd imagined. How was he going to unmask her?

Chapter Twelve

It was ridiculous. She should be home sleeping. Instead, she had gone directly from the airport to the bank. There was no reason to think she would spot anything unusual in Matt's code. After all, she had reviewed it Friday morning. Their best chance of finding the error was to do a standard code review with Matt and Sam explaining to Betsy and Judith why they had made the changes they did. That approach, Judith knew from experience, often helped programmers discover flaws in their logic. Still, the stubborn part of her didn't want to wait until ten when she and the team had agreed to meet. Maybe she could find the answer before then. And maybe working on the program would help her forget Glenn Hibbard.

It was absurd that she was jealous of herself. Judith had told herself that a thousand times on the flight home. Lynette, as Melinda had pointed out, was part of Judith. What bothered her was that Glenn was so attracted to her. Though he saw Judith almost every day and knew her far better than he did Lynette, he still harbored a fascination for Lynette. Fascination? It was more like an obsession. Judith knew she shouldn't be surprised. All her life she had known that men did not find her fascinating. Lynette, who was undeniably more glamorous than Judith, appealed to Glenn in ways that conservative Judith never could.

She wouldn't think about it. The DDA problem was much more important than Glenn's fascination with a certain English author. She would solve the rounding problem. But though Judith reviewed the programs, reran the tests, and compared the results, she could not find the cause of the discrepancy. By the time Matt and Sam arrived, she had begun to doubt her eyes. How could two sets of identical instructions produce varying results?

"Isn't Betsy coming?" Judith asked when the men had poured their coffee.

Sam shook his head. "Matt and I didn't want to worry you on Friday, but she didn't come in. We thought she might have the flu like Tony, so we called her house. No one answered."

Judith tried not to frown. That didn't sound like Betsy. Though she had come in late a few Monday mornings, she was normally a conscientious employee. She always called in when she was sick.

"I think she's out on the boat." Matt took a long swallow of coffee, then grimaced.

Judith managed a small smile. The bank's coffee

never improved. "Boat?" she prompted. Though she had heard about Betsy's new sports car, there had been no mention of boats.

"She told us last week that she was gonna get one. Matt and I figured she was joking. After all, where would she get the money to buy both a car and a yacht?"

Where indeed? Judith grimaced, wondering how Betsy would afford hefty installment payments if her job were eliminated. Feeling a bit like Scarlett O'Hara, Judith told herself she'd worry about that tomorrow. What mattered today was finding the reason her team's test results varied.

Six hours later Judith had to admit defeat. "We'll work on it tomorrow," she told Matt and Sam as they left the bank.

Tomorrow might be another day, but it wasn't one Judith wanted to experience. Not only would she have to tell Tony there was a chance they wouldn't have the new program ready for Excelsior, but she would also have to see Glenn again.

He opened the freezer door and stared. Though it was filled with his favorite foods, tonight nothing looked appealing. How did he get himself into these predicaments, Glenn wondered as he pulled a frozen entree from its box and slid it into the microwave. Last night he had been sitting in a revolving restaurant high above Atlanta, eating gourmet food with Lynette. Two nights before that he and Judith had been at the plantation, gazing at the stars and . . . Glenn forced his thoughts away from that night and concentrated on breaking lettuce into small pieces as if his very life depended on it. Though his eyes focused on crisp iceberg lettuce, his mind saw Judith's face, her soft smile as they walked from the restored plantation and the delightful flush she wore when they kissed. She had been the picture of a woman in love.

Love. Glenn had never put much stock in that particular four-letter word. Love was what the poets described. It was something that existed in books and movies. It wasn't something that happened in real life, and it most definitely wasn't something that happened to Glenn Hibbard.

He pulled a container of mushrooms from the refrigerator and began to wash them. If only he could eradicate the bitter memories as easily as he removed dirt from the soft fungus. He had thought he had loved Michelle, and for a while they had been happy. He hadn't imagined that. But then Michelle's love had died. Or had he done something to kill it? Glenn wasn't sure. Perhaps Michelle was right, and they had never been in love, that only she and Jared had known that magical state. All Glenn knew was that Michelle had turned from a radiantly happy woman into one who had cried in despair, a woman who had somehow lost control of her car and died. He couldn't let that happen again.

Glenn gazed at the salad he'd so carefully arranged. Though it looked delicious, his appetite had vanished. With one quick stroke, he dumped the salad into the disposal, then reached for the phone.

"Jared? We've got to talk."

* * *

Her first meeting with Glenn wasn't until afternoon, and by then Judith was prepared, or at least as prepared as she would ever be. She would talk about work and—unless he brought it up—she would make no reference to Atlanta. Melinda would call it cowardice. So what? This was a matter of survival.

Judith pulled out the folder with the notes she had made. When the team was unable to resolve it yesterday, Judith had realized she would have to tell Glenn about the problem they were having with the DDA calculation. Though it was possible he would think she was exaggerating, that this was a ruse designed to prove that the system was too complex to be outsourced, Judith wouldn't hide the problem from him, no matter what Tony said. When Judith had spoken with her boss this morning, he had sounded so ill that she hadn't told him about the problem. In his current state, Tony would be no help in resolving it, and it seemed cruel to worry him. Maybe by the time he returned, she would have found the answer.

The professional side of Judith was ready to meet with Glenn. The personal side wanted to be on a plane heading to Antarctica, New Zealand, anywhere where Glenn wouldn't find her. She could prepare to discuss business. What she couldn't rehearse was her reaction to the man who didn't love her, the man who loved Lynette.

"Good afternoon, Judith," he said as he entered the conference room that had become their second home. It had to be her imagination. You couldn't tell a man's

mood in only three words. It was simply her over-
active imagination that thought his voice was cool. But
as he took a seat opposite her, Judith's spirits began
to plummet. It couldn't be coincidence. Glenn always
sat next to her so they could look at documents at the
same time. Not since the first days of the study had
he sat on the opposite side of the table. Since he'd
done it today, there had to be a reason, and Judith
doubted it was one she wanted to hear. Seeing Lynette
again had convinced Glenn that the woman he loved
was the pretty author, not the plain banker.

"I met with Alan this morning," Glenn said, referring to the partner in charge of the study. "We talked
about the revised schedule. As you can see," he said,
handing her a sheet of paper, "I've compressed the
dates the way you and I discussed. Unless you foresee
a problem, Alan will call Tony tomorrow to review
the new schedule with him."

"Actually, there may be a problem." It was surely
Judith's imagination that Glenn's surprise looked
feigned. He couldn't have known about the test failure.
Perhaps he thought she was inventing a crisis to delay
or even derail the outsourcing.

But when she finished explaining the discrepancy in
the rounding calculation, Glenn's eyebrows rose. He
stared at her for a long moment, then tossed his folders
back into his briefcase. "Let's get out of here."

"I beg your pardon."

"We've got to talk, Judith, and this is not the place."

Minutes later they were in his car, headed north on
the parkway. Judith tossed her briefcase and laptop

into the back seat. "Where are we going?" It wasn't, she was sure, to a hotel that had recreated the Nile for its swimming pool or to an antebellum plantation's restaurant.

"My office."

Though surprisingly small and windowless, Glenn's office boasted four insulated walls and a door. Unlike conversations in the bank's cubicles, nothing said here would be overheard. Glenn closed the door, motioning Judith to one of the chairs in front of his desk. Only after she was seated and he'd taken the chair next to her did he speak. "I'm glad you told me about the rounding problem. It makes my job easier."

Judith twisted her cameo ring. Glenn Hibbard was one of the most sensible people she had ever met, but today he was making no sense. "How would a rounding problem do that?" she asked. "You know as well as I do that every system has bugs. One problem shouldn't determine whether or not to outsource the system."

"There never was any question of that."

Now she knew something was wrong. Glenn was talking total nonsense. Had he somehow snapped from pressure and that was why he had come to Atlanta? "What do you mean?" Judith asked, trying to keep her voice low and well modulated. Shrieking her dismay would accomplish nothing. "Outsourcing is why you're at the bank."

He shook his head slowly, then ran a hand through his thick auburn hair. "That's only a cover story so I would have a reason to be asking lots of questions about DDA." Glenn paused, and she saw the hesitation reflected in his eyes. "I shouldn't be telling you this, but I think we can help each other." He leaned forward, closing the distance between them. Though his hands did not touch hers, Judith could feel their warmth. What kind of help did he have in mind?

"Judith," he said slowly, "someone's been embezzling your bank." She flinched as if he had struck her. Embezzlement! Who would do that? "It seems to be a classic salami scam," Glenn continued, "with fractions of pennies diverted to the thief's account. The problem you're having with the rounding calculation points to that."

She knew the blood had drained from her face. What Glenn suggested was preposterous. First he claimed there was an embezzler at work, and now he was implying that it was someone on her team. He was wrong. He had to be. "I've seen the rounding code," she told him. "It doesn't divert the fractions."

Glenn shook his head. "Somehow, that program is truncating instead of rounding. We know that at least some of the accounts are being shorted." Quickly, Glenn explained about the conscientious controller who had discovered the discrepancy. "I've checked the numbers myself, and there's no doubt that those accounts are wrong."

Judith stared at the rubber tree in the corner, trying to marshal her thoughts. "You think someone on my team did it." She still couldn't believe the accusation. These were people she had hired. She knew them almost as well as she did Melinda, and she couldn't believe any one of them was an embezzler.

"It's logical." Glenn laid his hand on Judith's, as if he knew how shocked she was and how desperately she needed reassurance. He didn't offer any reassurance, though, only more of his irrefutable logic. "They all have both the opportunity and the skills."

That was true. "What about motive? Why would one of my team steal?"

For a long moment Glenn said nothing. He just looked at her, his blue eyes sober. "Money is a pretty strong motive," he said at last.

"I can't believe it. Oh," Judith said with a mirthless laugh, "no one's getting rich at the bank, but I can't believe they'd steal." Unable to bear Glenn's gaze any longer, Judith focused on the plant, wishing it could provide answers to a question she wished she had never heard.

"The evidence says otherwise." Glenn's voice was matter-of-fact. Judith kept picturing Sam and Matt and Betsy, trying to imagine one of them as an embezzler. The picture wouldn't form. "We don't know how much has been diverted," Glenn continued, "but it could be a sizeable amount. If someone wanted a new lifestyle, that could be a strong inducement."

Lifestyle. The word triggered unwelcome images. What little color had remained in Judith's face drained as she thought of Betsy's extravagant purchases. "No!"

Glenn tightened his grip on Judith's hand, his warmth helping to dispel the ice that had started to form in her veins. "Are you thinking about Betsy's car?"

Judith nodded. "And her boat and her jewelry. She might be able to pay for one, but she sure can't afford all of them."

"Unless she has another source of income."

That was what Judith feared. The other source of income. She pictured Betsy's face, glowing with pleasure as she described her new car, beaming when someone admired her jewelry. Surely she wouldn't have been so blatant about the purchases if she'd stolen the money. "I can't believe Betsy's an embezzler." Judith tugged her hand away from Glenn.

"Then let's find the account that's getting all that money. Let's see who owns it."

That was the answer. If they could discover where the pennies were being deposited, they would have a good chance of learning the thief's identity.

As she unzipped her laptop case, Judith wondered why Glenn hadn't looked for the account before this. Perhaps he hadn't been able to find an excuse that wouldn't destroy his cover. Interviewing the staff and studying programs made sense. Asking about specific accounts wasn't part of a normal outsourcing study and would have raised questions.

Judith closed her eyes, thinking. "If what you're saying is true, we're looking for an account that has deposits every night but probably has very few withdrawals." Glenn nodded his agreement. "I can write a query to find accounts with those profiles." Judith moved behind Glenn's desk, booted her laptop, and plugged it into his modem line. Minutes later, she watched the characters fill the screen. "There are twenty-seven accounts." It was more than she had expected.

"So, how do we narrow it down?" Glenn asked. He stood behind her, watching as she scrolled through the listing of account numbers.

Judith thought rapidly, then told Glenn her theory. "We'll catch whoever did this . . ." She wouldn't pronounce Betsy's name. The thief just couldn't be Betsy. Judith's fingers moved rapidly, keying in the parameters for another query. This time, the screen showed only one line.

She turned to look at Glenn, a sinking feeling in her stomach. Though his smile was triumphant, as the report confirmed his suspicions, there was a sadness in his eyes. "Who owns that account?"

Judith shook her head slowly. "Can you understand that I almost don't want to know?" she asked. "Part of me is angry—furious, actually—that someone would steal from the bank's customers. The other part is sad to think the thief could be someone I know and trust. I feel like I've been betrayed." She looked up at Glenn, hoping he'd understand. "Do I sound crazy, or does what I'm saying make sense?"

He nodded and perched on the edge of the desk only inches from Judith. When he spoke, his voice was filled with emotion. "I know how betrayal hurts," he said slowly. "It makes you doubt yourself."

Judith's heart skipped a beat as she considered the possibility that Glenn had recognized her at the autographing party and that he felt she had betrayed him. She bit her lip, wondering if she should ask. Though the cowardly part of her wanted to ignore Glenn's words, Judith pushed her fears aside. "What happened?"

He shrugged his shoulders, apparently trying to dismiss his pain. "It's a pretty ordinary story. The woman I was engaged to marry decided she loved my best friend."

Judith took a deep breath, wondering if this was the reason he had left California. Poor Glenn! Though her heart ached at the thought of someone on her team as a thief, she knew that her pain was nothing compared to what Glenn must have experienced. Even the anguish she had suffered, knowing Glenn preferred flirtatious Lynette to her, paled against the discovery that Glenn's fiancée wanted to marry his friend. "I'm so sorry," she said. This time she placed her hand on top of his, trying to return some of the comfort he had given her.

"I wasn't looking for your pity," Glenn said shortly. "I just wanted to tell you that I understand what you're feeling. Now, can you tell me who owns that account?" Though Glenn might claim that he wanted no sympathy, his abrupt change of subject told Judith the wounds had not yet healed.

She turned her attention back to her computer. Judith had deliberately not asked for the account owners' names on the previous queries. Melinda might call it cowardice, but Judith hadn't wanted to know the identity any sooner than she had to. She ran another quick query, this time asking for the customer's name. When the results were displayed, she smiled. "Joseph Reklaw," she read. Not Matt or Sam or Betsy. A total stranger.

Glenn shook his head slowly as he stared at the screen. "I was so sure it was one of your team. They had the opportunity. How could this Joseph Reklaw get the money?" Glenn paced the length of the office. "Maybe he's a friend of one of them."

That was the logical explanation. Judith knew she was probably being foolish, wanting to exonerate her team when evidence—at least circumstantial evidence—pointed toward them. Still, she needed proof before she would accept Glenn's hypothesis. "We've found the account," she told him, "but we still don't know how the money is getting into it. We need to figure out how the thief did it." And maybe, by some miracle, they would discover it was a simple error, that no one had deliberately siphoned money into Joseph Reklaw's account. "I think we'd better go back to the bank for that." It was past closing time now, so there was little danger of encountering someone from her team, and the tests Judith had in mind would run far more quickly over the network connections than they did over a modem.

The parkway traffic moved at a snail's pace. Normally Judith would have been annoyed by the delay. Tonight she felt as if she had been given a reprieve. "I still can't believe that someone's been embezzling."

Glenn tossed a token into the toll booth and inched

his way back into traffic. "Did you think it only happens in books and movies?"

"No." Judith wasn't that naïve. She knew that fraud and embezzlement happened. That was one of the reasons the bank insisted each of its employees take a two-week vacation each year, to increase the odds of catching irregular behavior. "I just didn't expect it at Sixth National." She leaned her head against the seat and tried to smile. "I guess there is a silver lining. At least if there's no outsourcing study, my whole team won't lose their jobs." *Just the thief.* She wouldn't pronounce those words.

When they reached the bank, Judith printed out two programs. "Here's the rounding routine," she told Glenn as she circled a paragraph of code. "This is the old version of the program. Here's the new one. You can see that they're identical."

Glenn compared the two listings. She watched his expression darken as he realized that nothing, not even a period, differed between them. "You're right," he said at last. "I see the code, but it just doesn't make sense. There *has* to be a difference."

Judith shook her head. She knew Glenn was clutching at straws the way she had, trying to find proof. They had the same objective—finding the thief. The difference was that Glenn believed it was someone on Judith's team, while she wanted to believe it was anyone else.

Glenn had started to pace again, although the small size of Judith's cubicle appeared to make it almost as frustrating as their efforts to find the thief. "There has to be something," he insisted.

Glenn was right. Fractions of pennies didn't just move from one account to another without a program telling them to do that.

"Looks like we're going to be here for a while," Glenn said as he ordered a pizza from Mario's.

While Judith stared at the computer screen, as if concentration would make it reveal the program's secrets, Glenn began doodling on the pad. She stared; he doodled; nothing changed. Exasperated, Glenn tossed his pen on the desk and began to pace. "Where's Mario?" he demanded. "By the time the pizza gets here, it'll be cold. You don't even have a microwave to zap it."

Zap it. A distant memory surfaced. That was the answer! It had to be. "There's one possibility," Judith said. "It's called a super zap."

Glenn stopped his pacing. "And what does this super zap do?"

"It changes programs without leaving a trace. Tony was the expert at that." Judith frowned, remembering the midnight phone calls she and Tony had answered and the number of times they had had to zap a program.

The grin that lit Glenn's face told Judith he was as excited as she that they had a possible explanation. "So, how do we prove it?"

The phone rang, announcing the pizza delivery. "You get the cold pizza," Judith said with a smile. "I'll find the proof."

The pizza was stone cold and distinctly unappealing. Judith didn't care. If it hadn't been for the threat of cold pepperoni, she and Glenn might still be sitting in her cubicle, trying to guess how the program had been changed. Now though she had eaten better pizza, she was virtually certain she knew not only how the code had been altered but also who had done it.

"Look, Glenn!" Excitement bubbled from within her. "There it is!" She highlighted a section of machine code. "This command moves the fractions of pennies to a different account."

"Joseph Reklaw's account."

"Bingo." Judith looked at the pad with Glenn's doodles, confirming that the account was the one they had identified before. There was the account number. And there . . . of course. The pieces all fit together.

"Now we need to figure out who knows Joseph Reklaw."

Judith shook her head. Though she hated what she was about to say, she was sure her guess was correct. "I can do one better than that. I know who Reklaw is." She pointed to the pad. "Try Anthony Joseph Walker." Her boss.

"Walker?" Glenn sounded dubious. Then, when Judith turned his pad upside down, he saw what she had seen before. "Reklaw is Walker spelled backwards."

"Right." Judith ran a quick query, verifying that the Social Security number Tony had listed on the Reklaw account was his own.

No wonder Tony had urged her to attend the conference in Atlanta. When he had learned her team was going to test the new code that weekend, he would have wanted to be in New Jersey. Tony had undoubtedly planned to change the new program so that it would pass every test. Judith knew he would have succeeded, if Fate in the form of a particularly bad strain of flu hadn't intervened.

With a triumphant smile, Glenn picked up his cell phone and punched in a number. "We're going to nail the jerk."

Chapter Thirteen

The day had started poorly, and it wasn't showing any signs of improving. It was bad enough that this morning's traffic jam had made Judith late for a key meeting. Now Betsy was crying again. If truth were told, Judith felt like indulging in a few tears herself. It was silly. Both she and Betsy should be happy. As Judith had told Melinda on Thanksgiving Day, there was so much to be thankful for, starting with the fact that there never had been any intention of outsourcing DDA. That meant that Judith's team's jobs were secure. The worries that had haunted Judith from the morning Tony had told her of the outsourcing study had disappeared. She should be happy, or at least content. She shouldn't want to cry.

Sam, Matt, and Betsy had all been shocked by the news of Tony's crime. Though it had been handled in the bank's normal low-key fashion, no one had missed the fact that the men who escorted Tony off the premises wore guns. No one knew whether he would serve a prison term, but they did know he would never work at this or any bank again.

As she thought about it, Judith realized she shouldn't have been as surprised as she was. The signs had been there: the extravagant vacations Tony took every year, the constant calls to his stockbroker, the furs he had bragged about buying for his wife. Perhaps she should have guessed that Tony was living above his means, but when she had discovered the reason he had been able to emulate the lifestyles of the rich and famous, Judith had been both shocked and saddened.

The day of the announcement, Matt and Sam had been visibly relieved that the threat of unemployment was ended. Betsy had simply cried. Not just that day, but almost every day since then. Though Judith knew why she was on the verge of tears herself, she didn't understand Betsy's obvious sadness. Glenn hadn't disappeared from Betsy's life without a word, but he most definitely had vanished from Judith's.

The last time she had seen him was the night they had discovered Joseph Reklaw's identity. Even though there was no longer any reason for Glenn to come to the bank, Judith hadn't expected total silence. If he had cared for her at all, surely he would have tried to see her again. Surely he would have called. But he hadn't. And that, Judith knew, proved what she had always feared. Glenn did not love her. No man would ever love her.

Judith closed her eyes, blinking back the tears. She

would not—absolutely would not—cry. The intercom buzzed. Glad for the distraction, Judith picked up the phone. "Yes?"

"Lyle wants to see you," the department secretary said.

Judith slid her arms into her suit jacket and grabbed her leather portfolio. When Tony's former boss called, she came running, as did most people at the bank—senior vice presidents got that kind of treatment. As she waited for the elevator, Judith wondered why Lyle wanted to see her. Three weeks before, he had assembled Judith's team to make the announcement about Tony's dismissal. Judith had not seen him since then, which was a bit odd, since he had told the group that he would serve as the interim department head until Tony's replacement could be hired. Perhaps he wanted a status report today.

Lyle rose as Judith entered his office. Though no one would ever call him handsome, he was a tall, distinguished-looking, gray-haired man. Judith found that his warm smile kept him from being intimidating. "Sit down, Judith." He gestured toward the round conference table. "Would you like some coffee?"

The shyness she thought she had conquered reasserted itself, and Judith could feel her hands begin to tremble. If she accepted coffee, Lyle would see how nervous she was. She started to shake her head, then nodded. She could do this. She knew she could. She took a deep breath, thankful that Lyle's attention was on the sideboard where a carafe of coffee sat next to several china cups. A moment later, when he turned back toward her, Judith was smiling.

"You probably know that Tony had recommended you for a promotion," Lyle said as he passed the sugar.

Her promotion. Judith hadn't expected that to be the reason for Lyle's summons. She stirred her coffee with hands that were surprisingly calm. "Tony said he would." And if she hadn't fully believed him, there was no reason to tell Lyle that.

Lyle nodded, then took a swallow of the hot beverage. Judith waited while he placed his cup back on the table, wondering why he was being so deliberate. Surely he must realize how important the promotion was to her. When he spoke, his expression was solemn, and she felt her heart sink. If the news were good, Lyle would be smiling. "I had planned to approve the promotion," he said at last, "but given the current situation, that doesn't seem appropriate."

Judith gripped the handle of her cup as she fought to keep her distress from showing. Not again! She had worked long and hard for this promotion. To have it snatched from her twice wasn't fair.

"I don't understand," she said, placing her cup carefully on the saucer. If she tried to drink now, she would probably spill coffee all over her. "I worked very hard for that promotion."

Lyle nodded, his expression still solemn. "I know you did. That's not the point."

His voice was matter-of-fact, as if he weren't destroying her dreams with his simple statements. Judith tried to quell her disappointment. Shouting at Lyle or, even worse, bursting into tears would accomplish nothing other than ensuring that she never received that Officer's title. But, oh, how it hurt to realize she would have to wait another year.

"I see." She lowered her eyes and stared at the coffee cup. Maybe if she memorized the china pattern, she would be able to keep her emotions under control.

"I don't think you do." The hint of a smile in Lyle's voice made Judith look up. Yes, he was smiling. How could he be so insensitive? She stared at him, willing him to change his mind.

"You're angry and hurt," he said in that same calm voice. "You shouldn't be." Lyle took another drink of coffee. "Judith, Tony proposed to make you an assistant vice president. I'd like to offer you a position as a full VP."

A vice president? The blood drained from Judith's face, and for a second she thought she was going to faint. Carefully, she took a deep breath, then another.

"Vice president?" To Judith's chagrin, her voice broke as she uttered the words. "I don't understand."

Lyle leaned forward as he smiled. "I've given this a lot of thought over the past three weeks. Even though there were some suggestions that I should hire from the outside, I think you're ready for Tony's job. The question is, do you?"

Judith matched Lyle's smile. "Yes. Oh, yes!"

"Way to go!" Matt grinned and shot high fives into the air when Judith told the team of her promotion.

Sam leaned back in his chair, a mocking smile on

his face. "I hope you aren't planning to fill Tony's shoes." He looked down at Judith's size seven pumps. "I don't think you can do it."

"Good thing," Matt shot back. "We don't need another Tony."

On the opposite side of the table, Betsy sat, clasping and unclasping her hands. She said nothing as the men continued to congratulate Judith. Then at last she opened her mouth. "I'm happy for you," she announced, and promptly burst into tears. Shoving back the chair, she ran out of the conference room.

"What's wrong with her?" Sam directed his question to Matt. "You guys share a cubicle."

Matt shrugged. "No clue. The last couple weeks she's been like a stuck sprinkler."

Though not a pretty analogy, it did describe Betsy's mood. "Excuse me, gentlemen," Judith said, and went in search of her weeping team member.

"What's wrong?" she asked when she had escorted Betsy into Tony's former office and closed the door. To make certain they were not interrupted, Judith pushed the "Send All Calls" button on the phone.

"Nothing." Betsy's eyes were red-rimmed, and she carried a tissue in one hand, but she tipped her chin up defiantly as she answered Judith's question.

Judith shook her head slowly. "I'm not buying that," she said. "You're doing an awfully good imitation of someone with something very wrong."

Betsy stared at Judith for a long moment, tears trickling down her cheeks. She dabbed at them, blew her nose, then muttered, "I've been such a fool."

Judith knew better than to interrupt. She sat quietly while Betsy fished for another tissue and scrubbed her cheeks. "You'll hate me when you hear what I've done," Betsy said.

Without hesitation, Judith shook her head. "I can't imagine anything that would make me do that." Even as saddened as she had been by the knowledge that Tony was a thief, Judith didn't hate him. The crime, yes, but not the person. "Why don't you tell me what's wrong?"

Betsy's eyes filled with tears and her voice wavered as she said, "I lost a lot of money. I don't know how I'm gonna repay it."

Money. At least Betsy hadn't committed a crime or been diagnosed with an incurable illness.

"Why don't you start at the beginning?" Judith encouraged her.

Betsy blew her nose, then kept her eyes fixed on the floor as she spoke. "It started last summer," she said. "I went to Atlantic City on one of those bus trips. You know, the ones where they give you money to play in the casinos."

Judith nodded, suspecting she knew what was coming. The pieces to the puzzle were starting to fit. "At first you won a lot, didn't you?" That explained the car, the boat, and Betsy's jewelry. Judith and Glenn had agreed that Betsy would have needed another source of income to afford them. Atlantic City was that other source.

"It was so exciting, and I was sure that I would never lose." Betsy's tears began again in earnest. "But

I did. I lost everything I had won and more. Then when I tried to sell the things I had bought, I found out they weren't worth even half of what I paid for them." She sobbed. "Oh, Judith, what am I going to do?"

Judith reached into her desk for a box of tissues. Handing it to Betsy, she said, "EAP can help you." The counselors in the employee assistance program were trained to deal with situations like this. "They'll probably suggest you join Gamblers Anonymous, and I imagine they'll help you work out a budget so you can repay your debts. Do you want me to call them for you?"

Betsy shook her head, as if in disbelief. "Then you aren't going to fire me?"

It was Judith's turn to shake her head. "Do I look like a fool?"

When the phone began to ring for the third time that evening, Judith glared. If she had to talk to one more woman with a saccharine voice exhorting her to subscribe to a meat delivery service, she would scream. It was enough to turn a person into a vegetarian. Let the machine take this call.

"I know you're there," she heard Andrea say into the answering machine. "Pick up the phone, Judith. If you don't, I'll keep calling every fifteen minutes."

A call from her agent was one Judith never ignored, no matter how tired or disgruntled she was. "This had better be good," she said, as she picked up the receiver.

"It is. Believe me, it is." Andrea paused for a second before asking, "So, how are you?"

"Rotten."

Judith heard Andrea take a quick breath at the unexpected response. "Then it's a good thing I called, because I've got just the news to change that mood."

Somehow Judith doubted that. If being promoted to a job she had thought out of her reach didn't fill her heart with gladness, she couldn't imagine that Andrea's news would.

"Lucy read the proposal for *Silver Rose*," Andrea said, referring to Judith's editor. "She *loves* it *and* she wants you to turn it into a trilogy, *and* she's prepared to go to contract on all three books *now*." It wasn't like Andrea to speak in italics, but then this wasn't a normal conversation. This was the stuff of dreams, the fantasy every beginning writer had, that an editor would be so enchanted by her stories that she would demand more.

"That's great." Even to herself, her voice sounded flat.

Andrea did not appear to detect Judith's forced enthusiasm, for she continued. "What's even greater is the advance Lucy's talking about." Andrea mentioned a figure that made Judith's eyes widen. "With some careful negotiation," Andrea added, "we can do better than that."

"Knowing you," Judith said, with the first genuine smile she had been able to manage, "I'll get those careful negotiations."

Andrea chuckled on the other end of the line. "No

doubt about it. I've already warned Lucy that she's in for some tough bargaining. She invited me for lunch at Lutèce to soften me up."

"As if that would do anything!" Judith scoffed, for she knew Andrea's reputation as a shrewd negotiator.

"Actually, it will. It'll give me a marvelous lunch."

By the time she hung up the phone, Judith was laughing. It was only later that reality began to return and the pleasure seemed to evaporate. That night, for the first time since she had been a child, Judith awakened with tears streaming down her cheeks.

"Are you sure this is absolutely necessary?" Glenn demanded as he pulled the car into the fourth nursery. "Artificial trees are a lot less work."

His sister opened the door and stepped out. "Come on, little brother. I know the perfect tree is right here waiting for us."

"It's easy for you to be enthusiastic," he pointed out in what he thought was a reasonable tone. "You don't have to lug a tree out to the car, into your condo, and then out again for the trash."

Karen stopped. "Want to tell me what's wrong? You've been doing an excellent imitation of Ebenezer Scrooge all day."

Though he felt like Scrooge, Glenn hadn't realized his mood was so obvious. A month ago he had been looking forward to the holidays. That had been a month ago. Now he wanted nothing more than to have the calendar magically advance to mid-January, so that all this holiday nonsense would be over. Forget

Scrooge. Maybe he could turn into Rip Van Winkle and sleep through it.

"Nothing's wrong," Glenn lied. "I just think you should get an artificial tree and save all this work."

His sister raised one eyebrow. "Sure."

When the tree was duly settled in its stand and Glenn had strung the lights, Karen handed him an envelope of snapshots. "Maybe this will help your mood."

Though Glenn doubted anything would cheer him, he pulled out the first picture. A witch was dancing with a green dragon. "Your party," he said, trying not to scowl. That had been the start of it all.

"Aren't they great?" Karen rifled through the stack. "Here's your mysterious author." The photographer had caught her with a look of wonder on her face, as if she'd just discovered something unexpected and delightful. Though Glenn had seen Judith in many different situations, he had never seen that expression. There was something young and innocent but at the same time worldly about her smile. Glenn closed his eyes as the pain surged through him. He didn't want to think about Judith.

Seemingly oblivious to his mood, Karen continued to hand Glenn pictures. As if he cared! There was only one guest at that party who had held even a modicum of interest for him, and she was one woman he would never see again. He couldn't face the thought that someday he might hurt Judith the way he had Michelle, and so he had determined that the best way—the only way—to protect her was to make a clean break.

It was a good theory; what Glenn hadn't reckoned on was just how hard it had been to stay away from Judith. He missed her more than he would have dreamed possible.

"Okay, little brother." Karen nudged him with her elbow, apparently to get his attention. "I saved the best for last." She flipped the picture so that he couldn't see it. "Guess."

In no mood for guessing games, Glenn held up his hands. "I give up," he said without venturing a name.

"Spoilsport! It's you!" She shoved the picture into his hand.

Glenn stared at it for a moment. Yes, it was him, wearing that much despised armor. It wasn't fair, and Glenn knew it. As annoyed as he had been with his sister that night, he had only himself to blame for everything that had happened afterward. There was no reason to inflict his miserable mood on Karen.

"I'll get even with you for that armor," he said, forcing a light tone to his voice.

Karen shrugged. "Idle threats, little brother. That's all. The way I see it, it was a fortunate choice." Her words echoed in his head as he drove home, confirming his suspicions. A fortunate choice. Though Karen had claimed the armor was the only costume available in his size, at the time Glenn had doubted it. Now he knew he'd been right.

Once inside his apartment, he pulled out the two pictures Karen had insisted he take. He didn't want to look at Judith and remember what might have been.

Instead he stared at the picture of himself in that wretched armor.

Why? Why had Karen chosen that instead of a clown, a lion or even a dragon? Glenn sat on the couch and propped his feet on the coffee table, narrowing his eyes as he looked at the snapshot. A knight in shining armor. Karen wasn't romantic enough to see him as Richard the Lionheart, rescuing damsels in distress. Yet she had selected that costume deliberately. Why? A knight in shining armor. Glenn said each word slowly, trying to imagine the convoluted workings of his sister's brain.

And then he knew. He jumped to his feet. Karen was right; she had seen what he hadn't wanted to admit. Maybe, just maybe, he wasn't too late.

He reached for the phone.

It was far from the best day Judith had ever had. Though she wouldn't go so far as to call it writer's block, there was no way she could claim that the sequel to *Silver Rose* was going well. With *Rose* it had been Charles who had refused to behave. For the longest time, her hero had insisted on looking and acting like Glenn Hibbard. It had taken all of Judith's powers as a writer, not to mention the search-and-replace features of her word processor, to convince him of his proper role. But in *Silver Sword* it was Janelle, the heroine, who was proving to be recalcitrant. Every time Judith put the woman in a difficult position, Janelle would turn into a wimp. She would run away or wait for the hero to rescue her. She never once defied the villain. Instead, she wept each time he did one of his dastardly deeds.

Janelle was everything Judith hated in heroines. She was spineless. She honestly believed someone else would help her out of her troubles, and she was willing to wait until that happened rather than seizing the opportunity and turning it to her advantage. Judith hated reading about weak characters. She would never willingly create one. Why, then, was the heroine of her new book acting so absurdly? Couldn't Janelle see that she would never win Simon that way?

Judith switched off her computer and stood up. There was no point in staring at an empty screen or trying to force her fingers to form words she would only have to erase half an hour later. Spineless heroines! How had she created one?

With a sigh of disgust, Judith strode from her desk. What would Jonathan Stockton say if he met Janelle? He had been impressed with the feisty Lady Emilie Wilshire and had asked Judith if she were an autobiographical character. Though Judith had denied it, she had seen the skepticism in Jonathan's eyes. If he thought Emilie was based on her, imagine the inferences he would draw from Janelle!

Judith stopped, her eyes widening and a smile curving the corners of her mouth. It was so simple. No wonder Janelle was such a problem. The woman had no chance, not with the role model she had been given.

Talk about weak heroines! It was no surprise Judith couldn't create a strong character, not with the way she had been behaving. How could she accuse her heroine of being a wimp, of not being willing to fight for the man she loved, when she herself had been guilty of the same sin? She had sat back, waiting for someone else to solve her problem, when the solution had been within her grasp. She would wait no more.

Judith walked toward the phone.

Chapter Fourteen

W hat would he do when he saw her? The question had haunted Judith ever since she had invited Glenn to dinner. He had answered the phone so quickly that she would have said he was sitting next to it, had she not known how unlikely that was. Still, Glenn had accepted her invitation without hesitation, leaving the optimistic side of Judith hoping that meant he had been as lonely as she. Though the weeks since she and Glenn had uncovered Tony's embezzlement had been among the busiest of her life, her days had seemed empty. Her promotion and the book contracts, which should have filled her with joy, had left her feeling flat. The problem was, without Glenn to share it, her success was meaningless.

Judith chewed her lip. She missed Glenn—oh, how she missed his smiles, his humor, his quick understanding. But there was the very real possibility that

173

he hadn't missed her at all and that he still longed for Lynette.

Judith twisted her cameo ring nervously as she tried to guess how he would react when she opened the door. Would he be speechless, or angry, or would he turn away in disgust? Judith wasn't sure which she feared most. All she knew was that she had to tell Glenn the truth. One way or another, the masquerade was over. Though she had extended the invitation in her Judith persona, she had dressed in Lynette's strawberry blond wig, green contact lenses, and sea-foam green dress. Tonight Glenn would learn that Judith Barlow and Lynette Thomas were the same woman.

At the thought of Glenn's possible reactions, Judith's hands began to perspire, and she could feel a flush rise to her cheeks. Why couldn't she be like her heroines and display courage in the face of danger? They were invariably calm. Real-life women—or at least this one woman—weren't so cool.

Though her hands were trembling and the butterflies in her stomach had grown to the size of eagles, Judith forced a smile onto her face as she opened the door. The man she loved stood there, looking more handsome than ever. A green cashmere sweater set off his bright hair, while tailored wool slacks emphasized his lean frame. Though he kept one arm behind him in an apparently casual pose, there was something about the set of his shoulders that told Judith he was not as relaxed as he appeared.

"I'm glad you could come," she said. The words were ordinary, but she meant them. No matter what happened, she was glad Glenn was here. Before the evening ended, she would have the answer to her questions, and then she would be able to plan her future. There was a risk—a very real risk—that her future would not include Glenn. Though Judith cringed inwardly at the thought, she would be spineless no longer. The time for truth had arrived.

Glenn's eyes moved from the top of her curly wig to her green satin slippers. "You look lovely tonight," he said as he handed her the sheaf of pink roses that he had held behind his back.

For a second Judith stood speechless. Though she had tried to imagine every possible reaction, she had never considered that he would make no comment about her dress and the wig. Unless . . .

As her eyes moved to the flowers, her heart began a funny rat-a-tat. Pink roses. Those were the flowers Glenn claimed to have sent to Lynette. Now he had brought them to her. The suspicion that had taken root began to grow. While she considered what to do next, Judith sniffed the blooms. "How did you know they're my favorite flower?" For they were. While other teenagers dreamed of a dozen perfect red roses or a single white orchid, Judith's dreams had always focused on pink roses.

"Lucky guess, I suppose." Glenn reached behind him to pick up a large cardboard box. "Can I leave this somewhere?"

Mechanically, Judith gestured toward the coat closet, her mind whirling as she led him into her condo. "How long have you known?" she asked qui-

etly. For there seemed little doubt that she had ago-
nized over how to tell him, when all the while he had
known of her dual identity.

Glenn raised one brow. "Since Atlanta."

Atlanta. The momentary panic she had felt when
she had noticed the cameo as she signed Glenn's copy
of *Web* had been justified. Judith sank into one of the
soft chairs, unsure how much longer her legs would
have supported her.

Glenn took the chair opposite her. "I saw your ring
at the first autographing session." He looked pointedly
at Judith's right hand. The fact that she was wearing
the ring tonight was a conscious decision, not a stroke
of Fate as it had been in Atlanta. A flush of annoyance
colored Judith's cheeks. At the time, she had been
afraid that Glenn would recognize her because of the
ring, but his lack of reaction had convinced her he
hadn't noticed it.

"If you've known all this time, why didn't you say
anything?"

Glenn's lips twisted in a wry smile. "Believe me,
there were plenty of things I wanted to say, most of
them unrepeatable. I don't think I've ever been so angry."

He had been angry! He had no idea how *she* had
felt when he had wooed Lynette with flowers and a
midnight serenade. Those lovely romantic gestures
had wreaked havoc with Judith's self-confidence, convincing her that Glenn cared only for the flirtatious
author.

"Then you knew all the while we were at that restaurant Saturday night."

Glenn's eyes darkened at the memory. "That was the point of the dinner. I wanted to unmask you, but I wasn't about to ask you point blank. I thought I was being subtle." His lips tightened. "Nothing I did worked. You just sat there, cool as could be."

"Me? Cool?" Judith couldn't conceal her shock. "Not even close. I was so angry I could hardly speak. No matter what I did, I couldn't get you to tell me the one thing I wanted to know."

"And that was . . . ?"

Judith shook her head slightly. Not yet. She wasn't ready to tell him how desperately she wanted to know whether he loved her. First she had to explain about Lynette. Only then could Glenn give her an honest answer.

"I had planned to tell you as soon as the study was over." The scent of roses filled the room, and Judith knew that, no matter how the evening ended, she would never smell roses without remembering Glenn's solemn expression as he sat across from her. "Once we got back to New Jersey, we were caught up in the embezzling, and then you disappeared. I thought you never wanted to see me again." To Judith's dismay, her voice cracked as she pronounced the last words.

Glenn's hands gripped the chair's arms so tightly that his knuckles whitened. Judith bit her lips again, wondering what she had said that had disturbed him.

"When I had a chance to cool down a bit," he said, "I tried to figure out what had made me so mad. That's when I realized I wasn't angry. I was hurt." Glenn's eyes held a faintly accusing look. "I couldn't believe you didn't trust me enough to tell me the truth. Oh, I knew why you didn't want people at the bank to know you were a writer, especially with the outsourcing study and your promotion at stake, but why did you think I would tell them?"

Judith reached forward and laid her hand on Glenn's. Though it was warm and firm beneath hers, he made no move to touch her. Judith's heart sank. "I never meant to hurt you. That's the last thing I wanted to do." Her eyes beseeched him to understand. "Selling *Golden Web* was a dream come true." She laughed a little self-consciously. "I'm not used to having my dreams come true, so I wasn't prepared for it. I didn't know quite what to do or how an author was supposed to behave. All I knew was that no one at the bank could ever find out, or I might as well forget my career." Briefly she told Glenn the story of Sally Andress, who had been shunted to a back office position because of her waitress's uniform.

"There's a world of difference between you and Sally." His voice was cool, and Judith's heart sank another notch. Glenn didn't care!

"Maybe if you're rational, you see it that way. I wasn't taking any chances. That's why I invented Lynette." Judith rested her shoulders against the chair's high back. Telling her story was far more draining than she had expected, especially since Glenn was providing no encouragement. Judith had the feeling she was pleading her case before a hostile judge. "Lynette was just going to be a name on the book cover until I was invited to appear on the Stockton show. Then she had to become a real person. That's when I came up with this disguise." She gestured toward her gown. Glenn nodded, his face still impassive.

"I never dreamed that pretending to be Lynette would be anything other than a chore. I went to that Halloween party to practice, nothing more. All I wanted to do was perfect my accent. Then you arrived, and everything changed." *I fell in love.* But Judith could not tell Glenn that, not yet. "The time we spent at the diner was pure fun. It was so totally different from anything I had ever done that I felt like I was someone else. When I wore the wig and the contacts, I could do things that conservative Judith Barlow would never dare to do."

For the first time since she had begun her explanation, Glenn smiled. "Like Clark Kent and Superman?"

"Exactly. You can't imagine what a heady sensation it was." Judith leaned forward to emphasize her words. "I never thought I'd see you again, and then you showed up at the bank." *And I fell even more deeply in love.* "I didn't know what to do when you tried to find Lynette. My instincts said I should have told you then, but I couldn't, and it wasn't just the bank." Though Judith searched Glenn's face for a hint that he understood, she saw the same calm exterior. Only the fire in his eyes disturbed the otherwise placid façade. Judith hoped the fire wasn't still anger.

"If it wasn't your position at the bank, then what did keep you from telling me?"

"My friend Melinda said I was a coward, and she was right. I was afraid that you were attracted to Lynette because she was flirtatious, and I couldn't handle that. I wanted you to love me as Judith."

Glenn's eyebrows rose. "But you're both the same person."

He didn't understand, and it was so important that he did. Judith tried to explain. "Believe it or not, it's taken me a while to realize that. I always thought of Lynette as a separate person." As Glenn frowned, lines formed between his eyes. "I'm sure a psychiatrist would have a field day with the fact that I couldn't accept the other side of myself."

There was a long silence as Glenn appeared to consider her words. At last he took Judith's hand between both of his. "I thought I had done something to make you think I wasn't trustworthy."

It was Judith's turn to be surprised. She had never imagined that Glenn's insecurities were as deep as hers. She shook her head. "The problem was me, not you. I guess I was a slow learner, but now I know that Lynette is part of me. An important part." She looked down at her hand, clasped between Glenn's. For the moment at least they were together, and it felt so good. "Tonight is Lynette's last appearance. I won't deny that it was fun pretending to be someone else, because it was, but that time is over. Lynette has served her purpose, and she's going into retirement." Judith raised her eyes to meet Glenn's. "I've decided that my next book will be published under my own name."

"A Judith Barlow? That has a nice ring."

Judith's lips tightened. "It's a risk. I don't know how the bank is going to react, but I do know that I can't keep denying half of myself."

"For what it's worth, I think you made the right decision." Gently he released Judith's hand and rose. "This seems to be the night for explanations. I have a few of my own." For the first time Judith heard hesitation in his voice. Whatever he was about to say seemed to bother him as much as her confession about Lynette did. She watched as Glenn pulled out the large cardboard box he had brought with him and laid it on the coffee table.

"You may recognize this," he said, opening the lid. Inside, carefully shrouded in several layers of tissue paper, was a coat of armor.

Judith stared, bemused. "Your costume from the party!"

"Exactly." Glenn's voice held such a note of mockery that Judith's puzzlement intensified. Her expression must have reflected her confusion, for he said, "I think I told you that the costume wasn't my choice. My sister picked it out for me, and even though she denied having an ulterior motive, I didn't believe her." Glenn closed the box, then took his seat across from Judith. "You may have thought you were a slow learner, but I wasn't any better. It took me a while to figure out why Karen selected this particular costume."

He took one of Judith's hands in his, his blue eyes

serious when they met hers. "You weren't the only one who hid behind a costume. Karen was trying to tell me that I've been wearing armor, even if it was invisible. I kept a barrier between myself and other people because I was afraid."

Judith felt the faint tremor in Glenn's hand and realized how much this revelation was costing him. "You? Afraid? You always seemed so brave to me."

Glenn shook his head. "Then I must have played the role well, because the fear has been very real and very deep. I told you about Michelle and Jared and how I felt betrayed. There's more to the story. Michelle and I had a horrible argument, and we both said some awful things to each other." Judith bit her lip, wishing there were something she could do or say to help Glenn but knowing that the best thing was to simply listen. "Michelle told me I was only half the man Jared was. That's why she was going to marry him instead of me," Glenn continued. Though his voice was apparently calm, the way he gripped Judith's hand told her how painful this confession was. "I called her a two-timing cheat and some other unrepeatable names." Glenn raised his eyes to meet Judith's, and the anguish she saw reflected in them made her catch her breath. "I didn't mean what I said, but I never had a chance to tell her that. Michelle was killed in a car crash on her way home."

"Oh, Glenn!" Tears welled in Judith's eyes as she thought of the pain the man she loved had endured.

"That night haunted me. I knew I had hurt Michelle

when she didn't deserve it. Worse yet, I was afraid that I had killed her."

"That's impossible. It was an accident." Judith's heart ached.

"Jared said that, too. He also told me how hard he and Michelle had fought their attraction. They both loved me, he said. The problem was, they were *in love* with each other." Glenn tightened his grip on Judith's hand. Though her fingers ached as much as her heart, she said nothing and simply let him continue. He stared into the distance for a long moment before he said, "When I met Lynette and Judith, I didn't know what to do. There I was, attracted to two women at the same time. I hadn't talked to Jared yet, so I was still blaming Michelle for saying she loved me but wanted to marry Jared. I was just as bad." Glenn looked back at Judith, his blue eyes serious. "The one thing I decided was that I wasn't going to hurt either Judith or Lynette. I had to figure out which one of you I really loved."

Judith laid her other hand on top of Glenn's. If only she had confided in him, she could have saved him so much pain. But her own insecurities had been too strong.

Glenn spoke again. "Even when I saw your ring and realized that what I loved were two sides of the same woman, I was still scared. What if Michelle was right and there was something lacking in me? I couldn't risk hurting you the way I hurt her. That's what I told myself." He shook his head slowly, as if denying his own feelings. "Jared said I was crazy and that there

wasn't anything wrong with me. I didn't believe him."
Glenn squeezed Judith's hand again. "It was only
when my sister showed me pictures of the Halloween
party that I accepted the truth. I claimed I was afraid
of hurting you, but the truth was, I was afraid of being
hurt again."

He gestured toward the cardboard box. "The man
at the rental shop thought I was crazy to want a costume in December and even crazier to buy it instead
of just renting it for a day. Maybe he's right." Glenn
shrugged his shoulders. To Judith's relief, much of the
tension seemed to have drained from him. Though she
wanted to speak, to tell Glenn she knew he wasn't
crazy, she realized that he wasn't finished with his
story. Until he had reached the end, she would say
nothing. "Maybe I am crazy," he said, "but I decided
I was going to hang it in my closet as a reminder that
I don't need armor. I'm not going to shield myself
from true happiness any longer."

A glimmer of hope began to glow within her. Was
Glenn telling her about happiness because it was
something he wanted them to share? He continued to
gaze into Judith's eyes, his expression serious. "I've
learned the difference between loving and being in
love, and I'm not afraid to admit it." Judith's hopes
grew. "Michelle and Jared were right. There is a difference, and no one should settle for only half."

Judith took a shallow breath. This was what she
wanted to hear. Glenn had already said he loved her.
Now he would make every dream she had ever cher-
ished come true by telling her he was in love with her.

But instead of declaring his love, Glenn released Judith's hands and moved back in the chair. As the glimmer of hope faded, she swallowed deeply. She had been mistaken in thinking that they had a future together. This was good-bye. Glenn was going to explain that he loved her, but it wasn't enough. He wasn't going to settle for second best. He wanted to be in love.

As Judith opened her mouth, Glenn shook his head, forestalling her. Sliding off the chair, he knelt before her. "I love you, Judith," he said slowly. "I've known that for a while." She nodded, unable to speak for fear that the emotions roiling within her would come tumbling out. Glenn smiled softly, as if he somehow sensed her confusion. "I love you," he repeated, "and now I know that I'm in love with you too. If you'll let me, I want to spend the rest of my life proving it to you."

Joy stronger and deeper than any she had ever known swept through her. Dreams really did come true! Once again Glenn took her hands between his. His blue eyes reflected the love Judith knew was blazing from hers. "Would you consider making your next book a Judith Hibbard? Will you marry me?"

Judith's kiss was the only answer Glenn needed.

Harte
Moonlight masquerade